AF184996

For Helga

Christoph Werner

CASTLE BY THE RIVER

The Life and Death of Karl Friedrich Schinkel
Painter and Master Builder

A Novel

Editor Michael Leonard

www.tredition.de

German Edition:
Schloss am Strom. Die Geschichte vom Leben und Sterben des Baumeisters Karl Friedrich Schinkel. Bertuch Verlag GmbH Weimar 2004

Editor: Michael Leonard
Layout: Helga Dreher

© Bertuch Verlag Gmbh Weimar 2004
English edition 2020 by kind permission of Bertuch Verlag GmbH Weimar

Published by tredition GmbH, Hamburg, Halenreie 40-44, 22359 Hamburg

978-3-347-04274-2 (Paperback)
978-3-347-04276-6 (eBook)

Table of Contents

Chapter 1...9
Chapter 2...27
Chapter 3...41
Chapter 4...55
Chapter 5...71
Chapter 6...89
Chapter 7...99
Chapter 8...107
Chapter 9...115
Chapter 10 123
Chapter 11 129
Chapter 12 139
Chapter 13 149
Epilog 157
About the Author 163
Also by Christoph Werner 165
Books by Christoph Werner 168

CHAPTER 1

On September 11th of 1840, a small crowd of onlookers had gathered in front of the portal of Berlin's Bauakademie, the Academy of Architecture. Normally, any build-up of Berliners wouldn't come together without noise and coarse jokes, but today people were quiet. They looked at the two carriages that had stopped in front of the Academy. The few who were still talking fell silent and glanced at each other bleakly. The carriages belonged to two doctors, the Privy Councilors Dr. Horn and Dr. von Stosch, who had been summoned by Dr. Pätsch to help him in the treatment of his patient, Privy Councilor Schinkel.

The crowd waited hoping to learn something about the state of health, or rather the illness of their beloved Director of the Königliche Technische Oberbaudeputation, the Royal Office of Works.

Suddenly there was movement among the young Berliners sitting on the lower steps in front of the portal. They quickly got on their feet and stepped aside because the heavy door was opened from inside, and the three doctors walked out solemnly. Dr. Pätsch accompanied his two elder colleagues deferentially to their carriages, and the bystanders could understand some words that were exchanged between the gentlemen. They heard fever, renewed turgescence of the blood towards face and head, but couldn't make sense of it. But then, when Dr. Horn entered his carriage, closed the door and through the window turned once more to his colleague Dr. Pätsch, one could hear him saying loudly and clearly, "Well, dear colleague, don't hesitate to take the measures we've spoken about. A renewed seizure could mean the *exitus letalis*." With this he signaled to his coachman, and the carriage drove off through the milling crowd, following Dr. von Stosch, who had started before him. Pätsch returned to the building and the care of his patient.

… Always the canvas recoils when he tries to apply the brush. How can hope be made apparent if he doesn't succeed in putting the white dove into the painting? Brentano's smile was so friendly when he, Schinkel, had made a sketch in his notebook of Brentano's impromptu story even while it was being told. And now, in oil, almost ready on the easel, he can't reach the painting with his brush. The canvas recoils, he can't get at it, somebody is holding him from behind, embracing him with his arms, not letting him go. Ah, Herr von Bülow, Your Excellency—has long since died, the minister—the sphere of the artistic, which alone appeals to me, is of such a limitless extent that a man's life is much too short for it. I feel, with great regret, that in other circumstances I could have achieved more, but that I'm being inwardly torn apart by work that drags me away from my true calling.

Then, before he even started sketching, friend Brentano unwaveringly contended that the poet is by his very nature superior to the draftsman and painter since he can express himself more easily and in greater detail than the latter. And, to give his thesis argumentative force, he told his story to those present, among them Arnims and Rungenhagen, in as complicated and abstract a way as possible.

Nature takes possession of a manorial hunting lodge. A proud stag enters the courtyard that had been left by the lordly owners. Gropius was present, as he was often at those soirées in No 99 Friedrichstrasse and—as he was a painter, too, supported the idea from the start. There was no doubt that Brentano wanted to particularly show the outdatedness of a nobility long petrified, of a world where there was not even a place to bury the castle's last resident, the old head forester, because the ground was all rocks. Therefore, the painter let the boat with the coffin cross the river to the other river bank, to a world of hope and renewal under the sign of the cross, symbolized by the vines and the dove.

That was ANNO DOMINI 1815, when the usurpator had finally been defeated. As a reminiscence of the dictator's destructive intentions the castle looks similar to Heidelberg Castle, which had been cruelly made a ruin, as had been the cities of Worms and Speyer during the War of the Grand Alliance, started by Louis XIV of France.

Then, after his interests had long been directed towards other things, namely towards real landscapes and their description by means of the art of painting, Consul Wagener had urged him to paint Castle by the River in oil and thus led him once again into the world of romantic-poetical phantasies. Though he had to admit that he had never lost touch with the medieval world even when deeply immersed in Greek classicism. Too strong, too belle et triste is the longing for the past and the belief in the oneness of man and stone and tree and God, prevailing in the olden times. A witness of this is the Friedrichwerdersche Kirche, the church on the Werderscher Markt in Berlin. Royal Architect Schlaetzer and archeologist Alois Hirt had handed in first drafts. But Schinkel, at that time head of the aesthetic department in the Oberbaudeputation, had rejected their designs in favor of his own.

His Royal Highness the Crown Prince had wanted a church in the manner of the English Gothic chapels, a wish that had corresponded with Schinkel's innermost ideas at that time, as the Prussian National Monument for the Liberation Wars on the Kreuzberg Hill in Berlin, made of cast iron, bears witness to with its Gothic tapering turret, whose foundation stone was laid in 1818 in the presence of His Imperial Majesty the Russian Czar. But he had often tried to adapt the Gothic style, the medieval architectural forms and elements to modern times, to give them a more objective, even factual character. For example, his drafts for the cathedral in memory of the Wars of Liberation, though never carried out, shows his efforts to rid the Gothic forms of their tendency to reach upward toward the sky; and what is even more, the building has not a steep, but a flat roof as the Friedrichwerdersche Kirche has. But still, early Gothic architecture revealed something one could call modern in that it kind of opened up the buildings, displayed the forces active within the walls and roofs and vaults, thus involving the observer and making him a participant in the work of the architect. One only needed to look at how the vault thrust is visibly accommodated by well-designed inside and outside structures. The vaults themselves are supported by cross ribs and flying buttresses, hidden in older architecture, all allowing the creation of the high-ceilinged Gothic churches.

When painting "Castle by the River", he had long departed from his medieval phase and felt ready, within himself, to paint the Rugard from nature, because he felt he had to serve the present and the tasks produced by it. The Rugard, the highest elevation of the island of Rügen, was of special interest to him because it was like a bridge between the present and the ancient past, as there had been a castle there in which princes of the Slavic tribe of the Rani resided, from which the name Rugard was derived. Schinkel felt he had to pay his tribute to this fact because it showed the continuity of man's activity within, not against, nature, a thought that had always been close to his heart and which he wished to make his contemporaries aware of.

So, in 1821 he had traveled to Rügen, then immediately continued to Bergen, where he rested at a place that was recommended to him by one of his friends in Berlin. It was the former home for widows of Lutheran ministers, called the Pfarrwitwenhaus, and there he was served an excellent meal of rosefish with potatoes and various kinds of vegetable. But he didn't stay long because his imagination was captivated by the portal of the Church of St. Mary, but even more by a stone there the picture on which, some people believed, represented Swantevit, a Slavic deity of war, fertility and abundance. But the parish priest said that it is more probable that the stone was put there in 1168 as a sign of the final victory of Christendom over Paganism. Victory over the heathens, really. Since his adulthood he couldn't find any sense in such a memorial. Had Jesus Christ wanted his followers to fight and kill others in his name? Though it may be possible that myths and legends were invented inside the warm houses without regard to historical facts while outside winter storms raged.

In the same vein people were still talking about the maid jump on the Rugard. Long ago a hard and evil Junker lived on the hill. His serfs groaned under his rule, because he demanded their hard labor without regard to the work on their own fields. But worst was his preferred pastime activity. The villain was not content with the body of his own wife to satisfy his lust. His mind was set on something else, namely the maids and young women on his fiefdom. So once it happened that a young and chaste maid went for a walk on the Rugard to enjoy the view and fresh air there. Why she did that, knowing like everybody that the land around the Rugard was the favorite hunting ground of the evil Junker, nobody knows. Should she not have been working on the farm where she was a servant? But maybe she had heard the rumor that sometimes, seldom enough, the Junker had acknowledged the fruit of his sinful exercises and compensated the maids with money.

But even if the girl had had that in mind, she quickly thought better of it, when suddenly the Junker galloped up to her and got so near that she could smell his breath reeking of cabbage, venison and wine. Also, he stank abominably of sweat from under his leather things. He attacked her with false pledges of love and tried to kiss her. Finally, the poor girl couldn't think of another escape than with her last ounce of strength to wrench herself from his arms, run to the abyss and jump into the ravine. There her foot made a deep imprint into the stone. The Junker was mad with rage, directed his horse down into the ravine on a passable path and, the maid being gone, lashed his whip with all his strength on the stone. The imprint of the whip and the trace of the girl can still be seen and, in the eyes of the simple folk, bear witness to the truth of the story.

Schinkel loved this tale of courage and sadness and tragedy, though at the same time had to smile about the naivety and imagination of the people.

It was this smile that caused Dr. Pätsch, the family doctor, who stood bent over the sick man, to recoil; it almost frightened him off. For weeks the patient had lain unconscious, had then slightly recovered and now lay with open empty eyes, not speaking, not answering questions, nor moving a limb or uttering a need whatsoever. Though the need to relieve himself, soiling his bed, particularly in the presence of others, caused him great agitation. He looked around, breathed more quickly, moved hand and foot back and forth and finally satisfied his need with visible energy without demanding a chamber pot or afterwards indicating that he wanted to be cleaned.

Now he smiled, and Dr. Pätsch feared that the symptoms which had so worried his family before he became bed-ridden would return.

It was a loud, almost hysterical laughter into which he broke out without any reason, quite unusual for him. And he couldn't stop it whatever he tried. Once Pätsch had observed, when a sad message was brought about the death of a friend, something in the manner of the teller made Schinkel laugh, almost convulsively. He had to turn away from the party, stand in a corner and let the strong vibrations of his diaphragm have their way until he managed, after quite a time, to calm down. Thank God, this time his face relaxed, and only a faint smile, as if he remembered something pleasant, remained.

Footprints in rocks. In the Harz mountains near the town of Thale Schinkel had seen the Rosstrappe massif with the impression of a horse hoof which, folks believe, is proof of an old legend. Bodo, a giant knight, once followed the king's beautiful daughter named Brunhilde, whom he wanted to marry against her will. Brunhilde fled on her white stallion or Ross, but suddenly arrived at a deep ravine. Her brave mount leaped in a huge bound to the rocks on the other side, while Bodo the knight fell into the ravine. The impression of the stallion's hoof can still be seen, and Bodo gave his name to the small river, the Bode.

Sceptics, however, think that the impression in the rock is the remnant of a Germanic sacrificial basin.

Schinkel took all this in when he traveled in the Harz mountains, but his real interest was something different. He wanted to verify the natural or even scientific explanation that Johann Esaias Silberschlag, appointed by Frederick the Great, Royal Senior Consistory Councilor and Privy Councilor in the Prussian Office of Public Works, Section of Mechanical Engineering and Hydraulic Engineering had given for the Brocken specter. Curious, that this learned man had tried to reconcile theology and science, an impossible endeavor. But regarding the observation of a physical or rather meteorological phenomenon like the Brocken specter he was a real naturalist.

Schinkel, as Silberschlag had done, climbed the Brocken, the highest elevation in the Harz mountains, and, weather conditions being accommodating, observed the enormously magnified shadow his body cast upon the upper surfaces of clouds that were below the mountain on which he stood. He realized at once that this was an optical illusion created by the observer's judging his shadow on relatively nearby clouds to be at the same distance as faraway land objects seen through gaps in the clouds.

His wandering memories took him back to Rügen where with his drawing materials he had walked up the stairs of the church-tower and turned his gaze to the Rugard. In the foreground he saw the last houses of the town, then there rose—woodless and dominant—the mountain; to the right and left in the hazy distance the bay could be seen. He felt driven to exactly draw everything with the crayon as nature seemed to order him to do, though at the same time, he was now convinced, he couldn't avoid violating it by adding something of himself.

It seemed to him that their friendly dispute during that distant soirée was decided in his, the painter's, favor. This was not groundless as words are fleeting and, moreover, can lead one to superfluous embellishments, to long-windedness or even to concealment. But painting, and, mutatis mutandis, architecture, are characterized by invariability, constancy and thus are open to verifiable truths. Through their different means they are more strongly forced to express the essence of the objective world.

Brentano and Gropius were the last to leave and both of them had the wish to ponder the evening over a glass of wine.

"Let's go to old Heineken. The wine from the Palatinate that he serves tasted good when we were there last," Gropius said and so broke the thoughtful silence between them. After a few steps they arrived at the inn and entered. Old Heineken, stout and red faced with a leather apron over his substantial belly waddled up to them immediately for they were welcome and precious guests in these difficult times.

After the victorious entry into Paris and the restoration of the kingdom of Prussia the economy was very slowly and with difficulty picking up, and not many Berliners could afford drinking wine outside of their houses. The innkeeper was an old hater of everything French and also knew that his two guests had kept their distance from the occupation power. But he had not followed the call of the Spenersche Zeitung to contribute to the fight against the foreign rule by sacrificing golden rings, chains and other jewelry. He was convinced that others in Berlin, who had not hated the French with such passion as he, should go ahead and take their precious things to the authorities. In the meantime, he would serve them with wine and thus make it easier for them to be drunk with the hope for victory. There had been quite a number, among them many women, particularly from the middle classes and nobility, who had made their peace with the French and had invited them to their parties, because they hoped to gain protection and business advantages.

Still other rumors and stories were told among the patriots and those who quickly discovered their love of the fatherland when their flattery didn't produce enough concessions from the French. A certain Freifrau von der Goltz despite her high title didn't think it a disgrace to offer her tender body and everything belonging to it to a French colonel while her husband wore himself out in the service of His Majesty the Prussian King at Königsberg. Well, the consequences were soon visible, and the memory of the much lauded ars armandi of the French did not

18

help her much in overcoming the shame she had brought upon herself and her family.

"What can I get you, gentlemen?"

"Two glasses of the Palatinate wine we had the other day," ordered Brentano, while Gropius found his tobacco pouch in his coat pocket and started to fill his pipe.

"Something to eat, too?" asked the keeper.

The friends, who were the only patrons at that late hour, looked at each other and groaned in comic desperation.

"God forbid," Gropius answered for both of them.

The meal they had been given at the Schinkels' had been excellent and plentiful. Frau Schinkel was well-known for her good kitchen. Though Schinkel himself was no friend of rich meals, because he felt he couldn't work well afterwards. This did not prevent him and his wife from entertaining their guests lavishly. That night Frau Schinkel had served their evening party her favorite baked pike.

Gropius read with pleasure Frau Schinkel's recipe, which she had given him for the enrichment of his own kitchen.

When you cook a whole pike, it requires gutting and trimming. The best pike are those of about 4 pounds. Any larger and they are too coarse, any smaller and they will prove tasteless.

Scale the fish, take out the gills, wash, and wipe it thoroughly dry; stuff it with forcemeat, sew it up, and fasten the tail in the mouth by means of a skewer; brush it over with egg, sprinkle with bread crumbs, and baste with butter, before putting it in the oven, which must be well heated. When the pike is of a nice brown color, cover it with buttered paper, as the outside would become too dry. If 2 are dressed, a little variety may be made by making one of them green with a little chopped parsley mixed with the bread crumbs. Serve anchovy or Dutch sauce, and plain melted butter with it.

Time: According to size, 1 hour, more or less.

Average cost: Seldom bought.

Seasonable from September to March.

While Gropius was reading, Brentano amused himself by recalling an argument between Bettine, his sister, and Frau Schinkel. It concerned Schinkel's thieving cook. "The Schinkel woman had a cook for three years," Bettine had told him venomously, "and during that time the cook had found an opportunity to secretly open the desk and steal money, which was only discovered recently. The Schinkel woman was mean enough not to tell me this story when she recommended the cook to me. Now Schinkel, who had no idea of his wife's recommendation, told me in her presence that I should think twice before hiring that cook. You should have seen and would probably have enjoyed the Schinkel woman's embarrassment." Brentano wasn't so sure about the latter. He knew how gossipy his sister was and that she did not always knew truth from invention.

However, Schinkel's new cook seemed to understand her craft; she had prepared the meal so well that even Brentano had had his hearty fill, though of late, Gropius thought, he often surrendered to mystical and spiritual moods and no longer harbored the happy and sometimes eccentric spirit of the times of the Christian-German Round Table Arnim and Brentano had founded. Obviously, tending to catholicism didn't mean that one had to always and permanently renounce all physical pleasures, particularly if one was still in quest of salvation and the meal offered was so good and, what is more, even fish.

The host brought the wine, wishing them good health, as was the custom. The friends raised their glasses and sampled the wine.

"Did you notice today," Brentano asked, "how friendly Karl was and how gratefully he spoke about all those who had stood by him, who had helped him in his life and especially in his fast rise in the Oberbaudeputation?"

"Here you have said nothing new," Gropius answered. "There is something in our friend's make-up that makes him talk well of everybody and praise their artistic achievement without the slightest hint of envy, sometimes, so it seems, more than they deserve. This must have to do with his own excellence in all questions of aesthetics, for which he is responsible in the Oberbaudeputation. It seems that such extraordinary talents make one either proud or modest, and if you are conditioned like Schinkel, modest."

"Gropius, you are young and inclined to limitless admiration. Schinkel talked, I think, about everybody who had helped him and from whom he had profited, above all of course David and Friedrich Gilly, then Johann Langhans, his teacher in mathematics, Hirt, who taught history of architecture, Freiherr Karl Wilhelm von Humboldt, whom he had to thank that he could, in 1810, become assessor in the Prussian building administration and that he, at the relatively young age of 35, was made Privy Councilor. And of course, he thanked their Majesties the King and Queen. But now I'm asking you, whom did he not mention? And why did he not mention him?"

"What, friend, are you driving at?" Gropius asked with a reproachful look. He didn't like it at all when even the slightest doubt was uttered about his friend and patron, whom he had been close to since Schinkel had moved in with the Gropius family in No 22 Breite Straße.

Brentano drank from his wine and leaned back.

"You know, my young friend, that I have been looking at my own soul lately more closely than before, that is I have been reflecting on what I was told when I was young and more thoughtless. You know that I am far from speaking ill of our Schinkel and love him as dearly as ever, as I did in the days of our soirées and the Sing-Akademie of Carl Friedrich Zelter. But looking at one's own soul critically makes one aware that others might have similar problems. Excuse me, but there is no way around it."

Gropius became restive. In his admiration for his friend he didn't want to allow anybody to nurse even the slightest objection against Schinkel and forbid himself—and if possible, others—any censorious view. Because he was young and enthusiastic, he didn't notice that with such an attitude he did his friend no favor.

"Whom did Schinkel not mention?" asked Brentano again.

"I don't know," Gropius replied. "It could be anybody. You can't always remember all your life's companions."

"Heinrich Gentz is the man I am referring to, Royal Building Director and at 30 years old professor for Urban Architecture at the Academy for Architecture. An excellent teacher and architect, from whom his students learned a lot, including Schinkel. And Gentz valued Schinkel highly, proof of this is that he asked Schinkel's help in producing a clean copy of the draft for a memorial temple for Frederick the Great, which was planned to be built near the Arsenal, but due to the war couldn't be realized."

Gropius moved his head uneasily. "And?" he asked, "what of all this? And how did you know it?"

He called the host and ordered another two glasses of wine. They didn't say anything until the host had brought the wine.

"Do the gentlemen know," he asked breathing heavily, coming to his favorite subject, the evil French, "how much war contribution this French Emperor had charged our Prussia with? 120 million francs. No wonder that the gentlemen can sit here in my inn so undisturbed by other guests. Our national economy has suffered dearly, the state had to sell many of its demesnes, money at the highest interest rates had to be borrowed, taxes had to be increased." Heineken stepped nearer and said, now his voice low: "All this I know from my brother-in-law, who is a copyist in the financial department. Under these circumstances, is it a surprise that the king has no money for building, and that so few guests come to my bar?"

"Well, Heineken, now you have expressed your opinion and have even been right, let us drink our wine in peace," said Brentano.

After the innkeeper had retired to his usual place behind the counter, Brentano continued:

"Where I know this from is not important. You should rather ask me why I'm telling you all these details. I want Schinkel to be judged justly. And that can't be done by unreserved admiration. He himself wouldn't want that. And he would agree if he were told that Gentz and he had much in common both as humans and architects concerning character and ways of thinking. Just remember how both of them in their architectural drafts stress the significance of the environment of the buildings as an inseparable feature of their effect on the observer. Such agreement does not always lead to mutual affection. We often do not like those who resemble us."

Gropius became pensive. If this was so, practically a law of nature, then Schinkel couldn't be blamed.

"Go on," he urged Brentano.

"Well, when after the return of the Royal Family from Königsberg things started to move again in Berlin and Prussia as a whole and a little money could be spent here and there for small construction contracts, student and teacher all of a sudden had become competitors. And both of them handed in drafts for the extension of the Princesses Palace and later for the mausoleum for our dear Queen Louise."

"Gentz too?" Gropius asked. "Schinkel's designs I have seen, but of Gentz' I knew nothing."

"You know, friend, Schinkel was and still is head of the aesthetic department, which means he assesses the artistic quality of all the state's building projects, the public representative buildings, the conservation of historical monuments and the architectural projects of the royal court. Thus, he had and still has a decisive voice when decisions have to be taken about the acceptance or rejection of the drafts handed in, including his own. That is a great responsibility and makes high demands on one's conscience and aesthetic objectivity, the latter being, if you ask me, almost a contradictio in adjecto.

How may Schinkel have appraised the designs of Gentz and what do you think was his attitude concerning his own presentation?

Anyway, Gentz had already been tasked with the construction of the mausoleum when Schinkel, without having been asked, also handed in a design. Then Gentz died and Schinkel went on with his own plans for the Mausoleum, principally extending it on the basis of Gentz' plans."

Gropius drank from his wine and was silent. For the first time he got an idea of how complicated life and the relations between people and particularly artists could be. And one could not easily avoid certain situations but would have to find ways to deal with their complexities What, he asked himself, should a man do if he were in Schinkel's position and finds, rightfully, that his own work is better than that of others?

Such a man, Gropius concluded, must have an outstanding moral integrity, and he was sure that Schinkel was such a person.

They finished their wine, and Gropius emptied his pipe and put it back into his trouser pocket, because since 1813 tobacco smoking was forbidden on the streets and promenades in Berlin, Charlottenburg and Großer Tiergarten park, and one could be heavily fined for violating this ban.

They paid their bill, and the host saw them to the door, lighting the steps with his rapeseed oil lamp. They went home in the same pensive mood they had been in when they had come.

CHAPTER 2

Oh God have mercy and take these headaches from me. How else am I to work and finish what I am tasked with?

His Excellency had certainly read the list that he had sent him, virtually begging for relief from the almost unmanageable number of assignments weighing him down. Primary was the aesthetic assessment of all governmental buildings for the Oberbaudeputation, not to mention checking the cost estimates for the churches, for which he was also responsible. After that came his own constructions, which he either had to review personally or which he had to supervise. Then he had written down the manifold works on behalf of Their Majesties and of the Crown Prince. His work in the State Agency for Trade, as well as his membership in the Senate of the Academy of Arts took up much of his scarce time as did the furnishing of the Museum at the Lustgarten, the professorship at the Bauakademie and the honorary memberships of the Academies of Prussia, Denmark, Rome, Bavaria, Russia, Austria, Sweden, not forgetting the Royal Institute of British Architects. They all demanded attention and regular correspondence.

He got confused, how could he complain to the minister, who had long passed away, about the inspection tours for the Oberbaudeputation through all the Prussian provinces? And how could he expect from His Excellency an answer to his petition in favor of the complainant? The minister not for the first time gave him to understand that this was a conflict which he, Schinkel, either had to solve himself or live with, whatever the consequences to his health. But how could he escape from this dilemma stemming from his Protestant Prussian duty ethic, of which he was well aware? Our mind, he had confessed to himself and others, is not free if it is not the master of its imagination; the freedom of the mind is manifest in every victory over self, every resistance to external excitements, every elimination of an obstacle to this goal. Every moment of freedom thus won is blessed.

God knows that his obsession with work was not fueled by ambition, or a thirst for fame, though he had weak moments in which he enjoyed his good reputation.

The minister, however well-meaning he was, could not help him. Would it have been better if he had been able to deal with His Majesty the King directly, in person?

But at the beginning, before he became Supreme Director of Public Works, he was not presentable at court and could only communicate with the King via the prescribed, official channels, which meant via the ministry.

Fortunately, the influential and responsible position of Royal Cabinet Councilor, who had to oversee all correspondence of the King, was held by the sympathetic Daniel Ludwig Albrecht, who knew how to deal with his monarch. The king didn't like long-drawn-out and wearisome lectures, and Albrecht had learned to accommodate this trait by skillful and comprehensive summaries. Thus, he was able to make the King understand what Schinkel wanted for the benefit of the realm. Though, of course, Schinkel had to prepare the ground by keeping his letters short, by organizing them clearly, often summarizing and numbering the individual points. In this way Albrecht was well prepared to use keywords when talking to the King, a way of communication that the latter preferred.

The canvas came nearer again; now he must succeed. With infinite effort, which made him dizzy, he reached out with the brush toward the painting. He pulled and dragged, though arms tried to hold him back, and reached the picture and, behold, the first white splash of color above the boy in the vines became visible. He felt that something in his head was stretching almost to the point of rupturing, and the picture before his eyes blurred.

The Privy Councilor in Weimar, Goethe himself, had admonished him so kindly not to ruin his health by endless work. And then he had helped him in every conceivable way in the matter of the collection of paintings of the Boisserée brothers. That was one year after the King had ordered him to build the Neue Wache in Berlin as a guardhouse for the Royal Palace, his palace across the road, to replace the old Artillery Guardhouse. The relation in which Herr von Goethe stood with the Boisserée gentlemen was well-known, and he had had the great kindness to sacrifice a whole day of his precious time in providing him with information about the financial situation of the Boisserées, of their characters and the purpose and value of their pictures.

Your Excellency, for Berlin this collection would be of inestimable value because it would help to eliminate the opinion, prevailing in Germany and abroad, of Prussia as a mere military state that was above all interested in saving money. It seems to be obvious that the possession of this collection is essential for Prussia and her reputation, even if one takes into consideration the plight of the state after the Napoleonic Wars and the finances required.

The collection did not go to Berlin, though he had already sent a positive assessment there. The negotiations had dragged on, the finance minister didn't at all like the sum he would have to spend which was usual when works of art were to be acquired. Bad luck would have it that a wave of high prices swept over Prussia at the time, and the theater at the Gendarmenmarkt burned down. It was quite a tragic and at the same time ironic coincidence that the fire broke out during rehearsals for Friedrich Schiller's fiery drama "The Robbers". The costs for rebuilding the theater amounted to 200,000 thalers, this was the sum the Boisserée brothers were demanding for their collection of paintings.

His Excellency von Goethe, on whose intercession with the brothers he had relied, had had a coach accident on his way to Heidelberg so that he had been forced to return to Weimar and could not, as was planned, talk to the brothers. It was only ten years later that the collection was acquired by Louis, King of Bavaria, for the increased price of 240,000 guldens. Though he, as well as Prussia, had lost, Schinkel congratulated the Boisserées on their successful sale. Now, he wrote, he had to see how he could find another way to fill his new museum. But in a letter to friend and sculptor Daniel Rauch he didn't hesitate to give vent to his anger. The Boisserées are no gentlemen, they are not fair negotiators, they are spoiled children whom everybody flatters. They had pressed him hard, enticed him with the stunning paintings and driven him so far that he went beyond the minister's instructions as he had to admit in the end.

For yesterday, it was the 11th of July of 1816, Privy Councilor Schinkel had announced his visit. He sought advice of how to deal with the Boisserées. Goethe was not quite happy about the visit, because it was only a month ago that his dear wife had been buried, and the household was not quite in order yet. He hoped that things would change for the better once his son August would make up his mind to marry Ottilie von Pogwisch and install himself and his wife in the attic and finally provide the household with a new mistress.

On the other hand, the Privy Councilor from Berlin, at so young an age already an important member of the Prussian King's Office of Public works, wasn't just anybody. Besides, perhaps he, Goethe, could render his friends in Heidelberg a good service by mediating the sale of their art collection to Prussia. Collecting, organizing, safekeeping for the benefit of coming generations—how near he felt to the brothers in these principles. One must never forget that the past is the fixed point in the fleeting present, the fixed point not open to arbitrary and time-dependent influences.

Admittedly, the reason the Boisserées collected all those paintings was deplorably determined by the circumstances. Sacral works of art, particularly from the Middle Ages and the Renaissance, were in acute danger of being scattered, sold and degraded to mere objects of financial speculation due to the secularization in the Rhineland induced by the French. So already in 1804, the brothers began to collect medieval art, motivated as much by the desire to save it as to possess it. Melchior Boisserée concentrated on acquisition, Sulpiz on research. Soon the collection more or less determined the lives of the brothers, though Sulpiz also developed a new theory of the history of German painting in which he rejected the idea that it had evolved gradually from crude beginnings; he proposed instead that a refined medieval style, ultimately derived from Byzantine prototypes, had flourished, until the art was revolutionized by Jan van Eyck.

Goethe wasn't completely convinced of this theory, but had found it an interesting approach which could at least lead to certain insights into the history of art.

Soon the collection encompassed 200 pieces and came to Heidelberg in 1810. Goethe was convinced that Prussia, though badly battered by Napoleon, would be required to dig deep into its pocket to fend off competitors and purchase the paintings. Well, Goethe wished Schinkel and Prussia good luck in acquiring the collection and the brothers a sizable influx of money.

The offer Schinkel would make and which he, Goethe, had communicated to the brothers per express mail so that they could think it over before Schinkel arrived, contained additional benefits, which were so tantalizing it would be hard to refuse. Schinkel's offer included the sum of 200,000 guldens purchasing price, payable in eight quarterly installments from 1817, in addition a pension of 10,000 guldens a year until the death of the brothers, rent-free accommodation in Berlin as well as 100,000 guldens for a fund for maintaining, administering and transporting the collection. A huge price, which obviously the Prussian government was willing to pay, because Schinkel certainly was too serious and considerate a civil servant to exceed his government's instructions.

There was a knock on the door and the servant announced Johann Heinrich Meyer, Goethe's right-hand-man in artistic matters, who had been living in Weimar since 1791, working from 1806 as director of the Ducal Free Drawing School. Goethe had invited him to share lunch with him. Yesterday Meyer and Schinkel had had dinner at the Frauenplan, after Goethe and Schinkel had driven to Belvedere, where he had shown the architect the Russian Garden, which was up to the last detail an imitation of the Czar's Very Own Pavlovsk Garden near St. Petersburg. Goethe wished by this to discover what Schinkel thought about the English landscape gardens, a style that was characteristic for the parks in Weimar. Schinkel had expressed himself cautiously, perhaps because parks and the like interested him only in connection with architecture in a sense of supplementation and meaningful functionality. This became obvious when they passed the Roman Villa in the Park on the Ilm river and Schinkel asked to stop the coach so that he could have a close look. Afterwards he expressed his admiration for the Villa.

Goethe's general impression of Schinkel was that the young man regarded everything, landscape and nature and the changes man attempted to subject them to in a very positive way, sub specie humanitatis so to speak, though without trying to unduly impose his philosophy on others.

The kitchen at the Frauenplan, despite the interregnum in the household, had done what they could with good success. The left-over hare from yesterday's dinner with curry cream sauce, which Schinkel and Meyer had eaten with good appetite, had been warmed up for today, and red wine, spices and cream added to the sauce so that a good and inexpensive second meal could be offered.

After they had finished dinner, Goethe suggested a walk in the garden behind the house.

"Tell me, dear Meyer, how did you like the Privy Councilor from Berlin? I was told that last night you had a glass of wine with him in "The Swan", so that you probably know more than I."

"It can hardly be, Your Excellency," Meyer replied, "that someone knows more than Your Excellency."

"Generally speaking, that may be true," Goethe conceded, "but in this case our Schinkel has certainly told you something that he didn't mention when he talked to me."

"At first," Meyer replied, "he offered laudatory words about Your Excellency. 'A whole and instructive day,' he said, 'I spent with Goethe today, who received me with utmost friendliness. Being with him means that a bandage is taken from one's eyes, one comes to the fullest understanding about the most difficult matters, which alone one doesn't dare to tackle. He also succeeds in making one conjure ideas from deep within oneself which one would never be able to do alone. Moreover, he gave me very favorable information on Boisserée.'"

Goethe smiled. "This is something I also like about Schinkel. He certainly knew that you would repeat his words of praise to me hoping to benefit from them in the future. And if he was honest, and I am quite sure that he was, nobody can say a thing against such reasonable diplomacy. Now, is there anything else you can tell me with being unduly indiscreet?"

"Oh yes," Meyer said. "He soon started talking about architecture and gave me a little lecture on the principles every architect should stick to today. The most important principle ..."

"Let's see," Goethe interrupted him, "how consistent Schinkel is by comparing what he told me about the same topic. To provoke him a little I maintained that an architect is somebody who leaves his work behind like a bird its nest in which it was hatched and has herein the most astonishing fate. How often does he not apply his whole mind, all his inclination to create buildings from which he must exclude himself.

Schinkel answered that with all respect he did not share this dedicated—he used this word in order to avoid the word limited—view. The building alone is patchwork and acquires its full harmony only through the landscape in which it is situated, through the neighborhood, where the architect places it. In this, there is simply no exclusion of the architect from his work. He added that architecture should be taught in a way that the future architect will never forget the purpose of his efforts. He must always be prepared to give an account of himself, of the sense of the work, he must not enforce his creational desire like a dictator, but this desire must take second place behind the work of architecture and its function. Function and the artistic interact so that one without the other would not have the desired effect. And both, function and its artistic expression are the requirements of beauty.

Meyer was impressed. "Your Excellency, if I am allowed to say this, has given an excellent summary. So I can spare myself a recap of our meeting in 'The Swan', which would be inadequate anyway. The essence of what Schinkel said to me is what Your Excellency has just put together."

Goethe smiled. "I hope the acquaintance with this excellent man will be useful for all of us in the future. And now, dear Meyer, let us part until next time."

With these words he walked his guest to the entrance hall and said good-bye. Goethe went up the stairs to his study. His meeting with Schinkel and the conversation with Meyer had left him in more pensive a mood than he liked. He went to the window and looked down into the garden.

He had to overcome this gnawing unease before he could resume work on his memories. For this he needed ease of mind, because all in all he felt that "From My Life: Poetry and Truth", personal as it seemed to be, was at the same time a history of the intellectual development of Germany. No better service, he believed, could he render his countrymen than with the completion of this book. His thoughts went far back, to the year of 1775, when he came to Weimar.

He had not imagined that he would spend his life here. Rather it had been an escape from the circumstances at home, which had begun to hem him in and paralyze his will. Lili Schönemann, so beautiful and young and bright, your harmless coquetterie hid the noblest soul and character traits. And yet, too fast, too smoothly circumstances made you my fiancée. Life spheres and world views of our families were too different. The invitation of the Duke of Weimar seemed to come at the right moment and helped me to reach new shores. But the most exciting and fertile years were behind me, though I didn't realize it at the time. Welcome and Farewell, Götz, Werther,

Prometheus, most of the first parts of Faust, what has come since then that can be compared to these children of my early years? Servant of the Duke, of the state, how much time and anger, trouble, and strength has this position required in the unending squabblings with the court, the petty arguments, when I wished to realize something reasonable. Everything, my work for Duke and state, my literary productions—all had to be wrenched from a body and mind that had been endangered from the beginning. I had to balance this with a constant and careful attention to the hygiene of the psyche and a prophylactic instinct, which, because it was clearly directed toward myself, were regarded by people as coldness of the heart.

And the same people, talking about me and Schiller, say that I am the child of fortune while poor early deceased Schiller had got it so much worse. They forget how soon Schiller, the starry-eyed, awkward young man and poor but noble beggar became a clever calculating realist, who knew his position in society and the pecuniary value of his literary productions.

When the Prussian Majesties wanted to persuade him to settle in Berlin, he wrote a diplomatic letter to Beyme, the responsible minister, and made the bold suggestion to live part of the year in Weimar and the other part in Berlin, reasoning that he could thus combine the inspirations of the big city with the contemplative peace of a small town. For this he suggested the not quite modest salary of two thousand Reichsthalers a year in order to—as he wrote—become a citizen of a country that enjoyed the glorious government of an admirable king.

Moreover, he did not hesitate to view their fruitful friendship not only as a poetical bond but also as something which should be used wisely in an economic, that is to say financial sense. And fame, the ambrosia of any poet's heart, Schiller enjoyed to the fullest in the last years of his life. Fathers carried their sons on their shoulders so that they could see the great man and keep his picture in their hearts for all their lives.

How, he was asking himself, did he come to this decision to become the servant of a prince? Admittedly it had been comfortable, too, and grounds that one could in such a position effect changes for the better in many fields, were not difficult to find.

I felt how Schinkel, without saying it in so many words, tried to find out how I am coming to terms with this conflict. It seems that he is suffering from an overload of work and is in his subordinated position less able than I to reduce it. But I think he has more easily than I given up the existence of an independent artist and become a civil servant. Intelligent and astute as he has to be as an architect, he has certainly considered carefully the advantages and disadvantages of his decision.

Be that as it may, his influence on the art of building in Prussia and Germany will grow, and he will in his comparatively narrower field of activity be able to impose his style and will much stronger than I can. But still I urged him to be economical with his strength, and it didn't escape me how often he laid his hand on his forehead as one does to assuage pain. Though too much compassion is not advisable and would be too much at my expense. I have enough of my own to do. And there is no doubt that Schinkel has almost achieved his purpose in life, which is building, following his own principles. When he serves his king, he at the same time pursues his own ends, architecture, so that he is in the fortunate position that the state pays him, the artist, for what is close to his heart. There are not many who enjoy such circumstances. But there are not many, either, who are well deserving of such circumstances and generously pay back what is granted them. Goethe turned away from the window, took up the last pages of his memories to reread and then summoned his secretary John to continue dictating.

CHAPTER 3

Oh, Sulpice Boisserée, how his draftings had helped with Cologne Cathedral after His Majesty had ordered its restoration. That at least had been achieved thanks to Zwirner, the Engineering Supervisor. How I backed him in his career until he started to chase after his phantasies in restoring the historical Rhenish monuments and buildings! In Halle on the Saale river we were still of the same mind, though at times I noticed how differently Zwirner viewed restoration of what has been handed down to us. He wanted to preserve everything in its purest original style, unmindful of other, higher, classical considerations.

Something tugged in Schinkel's head, his eyes seemed to be pressed from inside, a blood-colored cloud passed before them, then he could see the picture again. The white splash was still there, he stretched out his hand and painted body, neck and head of the dove before the painting receded again, he pressed and pulled, but held tight from behind by those arms he couldn't get at it again, the exertion caused the picture to vanish from his sight.

The doctor asked for a wet cloth and wiped the patient's face. He didn't seem to notice what happened around him. Dr. Pätsch turned to Frau Schinkel, who stood behind him.

"How unbelievably fast, Madame, has this malaise come over our dear Privy Councilor. When I examined him two years ago, he only complained about his declining capacity for work. An amiable peace of mind and the remarkable serenity of his whole

41

personality, the absence even of the slightest trace of hypochondriac depressive mood was an almost comic contradiction to this complaint."

"Doctor, I don't hesitate to confess," replied Frau Schinkel, "that I and our family were more eager to get your, the doctor's advice than was Schinkel himself, who regarded his health problems as minor and as the natural consequences of approaching old-age."

"I can quite believe that, knowing our friend," the doctor replied. "But now we must do everything that is humanly possible to alleviate his suffering. Just tell me again what happened last summer."

Susanne Schinkel bent over her husband, carefully lifted his head and smoothed the pillow. Then she turned back to the doctor.

"After my husband had taken Dr. H. Meyer's carbonic bitter water here in Berlin for four weeks, more as a precautionary measure than because he really needed it, he traveled to south Germany, to Meran. He wanted to undergo the whey treatment offered there and also, he had said, enjoy the beautiful Alpine nature and get back health and strength. On his return journey he stayed in Munich for three days, where he worked incessantly on the improvement of two badly constructed houses that his host, the sculptor Joseph Kirchmayer, wanted to combine. Kirchmayer was duly surprised and overjoyed at this gift of an excellent construction plan. You see, doctor, that's quite typical of my Karl, always working, regardless of his health, and at times, of us, his family. Although I want to say that he, whenever he could, took us along on his numerous travels. But even if those travels were of a private nature, as our trip to Italy, which he was eager to show us, most of the time he didn't stop working."

At this point they were interrupted by the entry of their daughter Marie, a sturdy young woman, who was now pale and sorrowful because of the state of her father. She had brought a cup of tea for him. Susanne Schinkel, who often worried about her daughters Marie and Susanne—one year younger and named after her—both of whom were still unmarried, frequently felt neglectful because the misery her husband had to bear these days made her less attentive to them.

The doctor indicated to Marie that she could let her father have the tea. She went to the bed and said, "Papa, here is something to drink." When she tried to lift his head a bit and brought the cup to his lips, something quite unexpected happened that filled those present first with joy and then with horror. Because never before during his illness had the patient demanded something of his own free will, only in refusing had he shown what was left in him of energy.

If he had not been fed, he would have died of hunger; but if he, for some reason, didn't want to eat, he tried to evade the feeding hand by moving his head sideways, and only if this didn't succeed did he make a dismissive movement with his hand. But now, when he noticed that Marie wanted to give him something to drink, he called out, "Wait a minute, my girl!" and immediately began coughing heavily, which would have prevented him from drinking. Also, Marie realized, the cough would have made him spill the tea, which he wanted to avoid. After the coughing attack had passed, he took several small sips of tea and, without any further words, fell back into his former apathetic and motionless state, eyes open and staring ahead.

"I am afraid, Madame, this was just a singular event and no symptom of a general improvement," said the doctor. "And what happened next in the summer?"

"He departed from Munich in good health and arrived in Berlin on September 9th after a five-day rather hectic journey in great heat, during which, however, he rested during the nights. On the way, though, he complained about headaches and tiredness which had become worse by the last day of the trip."

What had he tasted just now? His Marie was there and the doctor, who had asked him in such an odd way if he recognized him. Why should he not recognize him? What had happened to him? What had they done to him?

The tea he had just been given reminded him ... yes, of Halle, the old tea room near the Marktplatz, the university, Zwirner, the Crown Prince, Moritzburg castle—the memories swept over him like waves and threatened to take away his breath.

Who had traveled with me—Dr. Waagen, medalist Brandt, August Kerll, did I show them the city? Why did I make sketches of the Marktplatz with the Red Tower and the Church of Our Dear Lady, of the ruins on the Petersberg mountain, of Moritzburg castle?

The headaches don't let me think clearly and date the events in their right order.

Did we come via Wittenberg?

At 5 o'clock we continue on our way. The Elbe river had flooded its banks and wide areas are under water. We drive on the dams, which with their bridges rise above the water. The bright morning let the large water areas appear beautiful and at the same time strange with the trees and buildings protruding above the flood. We soon drive through the water, which reaches over the axles and hear news from Dresden that the rising flood could cause great damage there. The owners of the land are building emergency dams to save their hay harvest. We reach the small town of Ragun, again through deep water, and have lunch there. In this part of the country we get excellent beer, fine butter and savory bread. The innkeepers only charge very moderate prices.

The way to Halle, because of the floods, demands detours and takes quite a time so that we arrive at Halle as late as half past nine. Before supper I show my traveling companions parts of the city in the twilight and the picturesque churches, which delight them very much.

Our rooms in "The Golden Ring" face toward the Marktplatz; we can see the warder high up on the bridge that connects two of the spires at the east end of the church. He blows on his trombone a fine choral with great feeling into the night and then retreats to his lonely dimly lit room.

We enjoy a fine supper and go to bed. The strong Halle beer and the voluminous eiderdowns make the night rather hot for me.

The smell of lignite peat wafts through the window. This peat has long been used by the Pfänner guild of the salt springs below the church of Our Dear Lady for heating the salt pans and has begun to be used in the houses and bakeries, too.

The water that the starch manufacturers of Glaucha let flow in open gutters through the streets of their quarter also smells unpleasant, and already yesterday I noticed how due to the bumpy cobbles brown coal dust rises from the peat wagons and covers this City of the Muses with a black penitential robe.

The 1st of July. I rise at three o'clock to evade the heat, take time with my toilet and feel splendid. After coffee I walk to the Stadtgottesacker cemetery on the Martinsberg hill, situated before the Leipziger city gate and admire the burial ground of Nickel Hofmann, the architect of Cardinal Albrecht, who designed it in the Italian style of a Campo Santo. There are 94 grave arches, which frame the roughly 13 feet deep tombs. They are provided with flat-curved wooden covers. The whole work of art, created by Hofmann and his stone-masons, has been admired without reservations from the beginning. I visit the resting places of Francke and Thomasius, and a breath of eternity rises to me from their graves. How would that be, deep, eternal, dreamless sleep without any pain and stressful trouble and sorrow?

I'm told that Matthias Grünewald was buried here, but I can't find his grave. After his grand perception of form and light he is called the German Correggio, which brings to mind the Isenheim Altarpiece, which leaves no doubt that he was one of the greatest German painters of his age, whose works on religious themes achieve a visionary expressiveness through intense color and agitated line. Is there anything today that can be compared with this masterpiece in southern Alsace from 1515? I don't think so.

The crucifixion is framed on the left by the martyrdom of Saint Sebastian pierced by arrows and on the right by Saint Anthony standing placidly though he is being taunted by a frightening monster. The two saints protect and heal the sick, Saint Anthony as the patron saint of the victims of Saint Anthony's fire and Saint Sebastian, whose aid was called upon by victims of the plague. One can also see the hermits Antonius and Paulus in wild, phantasmagoric surroundings and the Madonna in a rich landscape with singing and music-playing angels. Truly an outstanding master, who can justly be equated with Dürer.

I leave the Stadtgottesacker and meet with my friends on the Marktplatz, and until 5 o'clock we enjoy the interior of Our Dear Lady, which is also a work of Nickel Hofmann, at least its completion. Here the master still stuck to the medieval forms from the end of the fifteenth century, while he did the Stadtgottesacker constructions in a new character.

My friends are quite enthusiastic about the various picturesque corners of the city; I myself discover places with views that I didn't know before. There is one in particular where the water rushes out from the mills, above it the ruins of Moritzburg castle, the castle church with its round gables, and under it many private gardens with arbors and thick lilac bushes on and about the old walls.

The exterior of the other Moritzkirche, covered with beautiful sculptures, and the interior of the Marktkirche executed in a very individual late medieval style with a harmonic and daringly artful construction so well preserved, are met with admiration and pleasure from my group.

I lead the party to the Alter Markt and show them the cannon ball embedded in the wall of the corner house No 26. Underneath we read the words, carved in a stone slab: Gedenke Schmidt, 28. April 1813.

My companions give voice to all kinds of assumptions as to what sort of romantic secret could be hidden behind these words.

After letting them guess for a while I repeat to them what our landlord had told me yesterday.

During the spring campaign in 1813 against Napoleon an advancing corps under General Lauriston had marched to the west bank of the Saale river between the vineyards and the village of Passendorf, and on April 28 bombarded the city of Halle from 3 o'clock in the afternoon.

Among other damage one spire of Our Dear Lady on the Marktplatz was hit. And a further bomb hit this corner house in front of us. Unperturbed by the bombardment the owner of the house and his family were having their afternoon coffee in the dining room. Herr Schmidt, the father of the family, was just on the point of explaining to his family that due to the position of the cannons and the launching angle as well as the direction of the wind they were safe, when a stone cannon ball flew through the open window and got stuck in the opposite wall. Out of gratefulness for this miraculous salvation and to the satisfaction of his wife Schmidt after the end of the war had the cannon ball built into the outer wall and the stone slab fixed under it.

We relate to each other further examples of unbelievable salvations and walk at a leisurely pace to the point of departure for the coach.

There the coachman tells us surprisingly that he would leave us to another, younger colleague, who hitches fresh horses to our coach.

Do we continue via Seeburg and Eisleben? What happens to the university, has Zwirner built it? Why did the King not accept my project, despite the pleading of His Royal Highness the Crown Prince, to use Moritzburg castle for the university? I can't answer the questions, my senses are confused, my neck hurts too much, will the doctor again cut into the boil with the lancet of which I hear him talk?

There were a number of good reasons to use Moritzburg castle, first its attractive location, then the fact that the riding arena, library, physical and chemical laboratory, zoological and mineralogical cabinet and, most important, maternity hospital are near.

His Royal Highness was very much in favor, because he harbored strong feelings for Halle. Our Queen Louise had often told the Crown Prince of the memorable hours which she had spent with the King in Giebichenstein castle and its park in July 1799. And when the administrative district of Giebichenstein was turned into a royal demesne in 1813, the King allocated it to the Crown Prince.

At that time the Crown Prince, art-loving and open to all kinds of romantic ideas, had resolved not only to take the castle but all other old art monuments of Halle and its surroundings under his patronage.

For example, he tried to prevent the demolition of the Steintor city gate, though in vain, and arranged for the restoration of the old church in Landsberg and the ruins on Petersberg mountain, of which I made sketches.

His Royal Highness was kind enough to ascribe the idea of turning Moritzburg castle into a university building to me, though he himself could rightly have claimed authorship of the idea.

The governor of the province of Magdeburg, Herr von Klewitz had let me read the letter in which His Highness wrote,

"As now the plan has come into view that a university building is to be erected in Halle, Privy Councilor Schinkel asked if it should not be possible to restore the almost completely ruined Moritzburg castle and make it usable for that purpose. With this an idea was put into words that I had entertained earlier and whose realization agrees with me very much. Information gathered around the location reveals that this beautiful old building has been in the hands of hereditary tenants, who are responsible for its ruination, partly by neglect and partly by intention."

His Royal Highness, the dear fool, developed an artistry and talent for drawing, motivated by Rauch and myself, but ended up more and more in that medieval-romantic world of ideas that will probably, as soon as he will accede to the throne, place him under the influence of orthodox and ultramontane advisers.

Well, the Moritzburg was a good choice, and Minister Altenstein had to remind me to finally deliver the drafts and cost estimates – which for lack of time I hadn't done – for the Moritzburg project. Among them was the large overall perspective view, because the layman would not be able to get an idea of the effects of the whole building from the purely architectural drawings. I also described the advantages compared to a completely new building, because here one wouldn't be forced to stick to a perfect symmetry, but could make use of the picturesqueness that an old building of this kind features.

The project came to nothing due to the incalculable costs, the negotiations with the hereditary tenants and the necessity of finding other locations for the military and saline authorities.

People had quickly raised objections. My design would mean too strong an alteration of the late medieval building. What in the opinion of those people does restoration mean? Recreation of the old without regard to the needs of the present? The most exact renewal of the past, though its function does not longer exist? Repair of the empty shell as it once was without being able to recall the spirit and task for which it was once built? Production of lifeless museum pieces in a surrounding for which they no longer have any use and with which they can therefore not interact? Or with which they can only interact in a very contradictory and anachronistic way?

No, retain the past and preserve it in the present, fill it with life, let it function in a fitting, up-to-date relationship to the surroundings and the polis, that's what I call restoration. It would confer on Moritzburg castle something of a future when students study in its rooms and recognize in the old building that the present cannot exist without the past, but the past without the present is but a sounding gong or a clanging symbol, a thing without real love.

Preservation of all monuments and antiquities of our country, as I have written down in a letter accompanying my opinion about the All Saints' or Castle Church in Wittenberg, is now, after the disadvantageous circumstances in our country have ended, the most important point of our considerations, which must concentrate on the renewal of life and activity for the spiritual and emotional needs of the people.

The same was true of my design for the Royal Palace on the Acropolis of Athens, which I was entrusted with in 1834. As late as the last century it was customary to adapt even historically hallowed places high-handedly. In my design for the Acropolis I leave the ruins untouched and still achieve a balance that is meant to symbolize the practical government of the king.

Oh God that hurt, somebody is lifting my head, my arm, voices are reaching my ear, I want to fend them off, why don't they let me lie in peace, what are they doing, they are cutting into my arm, I feel giddy.

Such a sudden turn for the worse had not been expected. Dr. Pätsch had summoned the surgeon in order to bleed the patient because he was afraid of another apoplectic fit. During the half-hour that remained until they could expect the surgeon, a messenger of His Majesty, a close friend of the patient of many years, arrived to find out about his state. And all of a sudden Schinkel changed noticeably. The same man, who just one minute before had been unable to say a sentence without leaving out whole words, who had lain in his bed apathetically, straightened up, joy and interest enlivened his face, and he and the messenger began a talk that lasted a quarter of an hour, about the trip to Munich and the art scene there, about artists they both knew and many other things, so full of life and intellectually stimulating that the doctor, who viewed the scene from the window, didn't trust his senses and made him doubt the wisdom of a blood-letting.

But hardly had the visiting friend turned his back and left and the surgeon had entered, the patient fell back into his previous apathetic state, so that now the doctors started the bleeding. The surgeon opened the vein with his lancet and took about 14 ounces of blood. While the wound was patched up the patient passed out and only after a while recovered slightly but did not regain the capacity to communicate.

CHAPTER 4

His Majesty had invited for dinner. University Chancellor Niemeyer was visiting his friend Bishop Dr. Eylert, member of the State Council and the Ministry of Spiritual and Educational Affairs, to ask for his help in the matter of the university building in Halle. He had hoped that Eylert would make it possible for Niemeyer to personally plead for his plans with the monarch.

On April 18th 1827, the Chancellor was to have his 50th anniversary of academic service. The City and University in Halle were preparing for the ceremony. For the chancellor the forthcoming festival seemed to be a good chance to personally present "the matter" to the King. "The matter" was the construction of a new modern university building instead of the old school church that had been used until then.

He had asked for a private audience, which the King had not granted. Instead, which was just as well, he had ordered Niemeyer and Eylert to attend the midday meal at the Crown Prince's Palace, which the King had moved into when he was sixteen and still Crown Prince. The meal was modest, because Frederick William had been unpretentious all his life. After the carrot and orange soup there was spiked venison roast with cranberries and finally an apricot compote and strawberry parfait. Various wines from the Saale and Unstrut rivers and from the Rhine were offered. Niemeyer, despite his age, had a refreshingly good appetite, as his friend Eylert remarked, and served himself cheerfully and without unnecessary restraint.

The King, who was quite observant, said with a smile, "Hope he gets enough to eat in Halle. Remember having been fed well in "The Moor" in Giebichenstein." He hardly ever spoke in complete sentences.

"Thank you, Your Majesty," Niemeyer replied, "if everything in Halle were so abundant as the food, we would be happier."

"How mean?" the King asked.

"Well," Niemeyer said, "Your Majesty certainly knows about the financial difficulties of the university and the urgency for a new sufficiently large building."

The King made no comment on this remark but turned to Eylert with a question regarding church problems.

But Niemeyer, unimpressed or rather mindful of his "matter" and sitting opposite the King, employed his well-known talent for a witty and charming conversation. Following up remarks by the royal host which related to Halle he entertained the party with anecdotes from his deportation, which he, nolens volens, had to suffer as hostage of the French, talked about the charter of Oxford University and other interesting topics. In short, he captivated the whole dinner party.

After he had risen from the table, the King approached the friends Eylert and Niemeyer and said, "Entertained me pleasantly. Thank you! Brought something?"

"Oh," replied the chancellor, "I didn't bring anything, but would like to ask for a royal favor."

"Well, and what?"

And now Niemeyer, in a deferential but still dignified manner and with a low voice stated his request with such alluring arguments that the King seemed to visibly be impressed.

All the more unexpected was his sonorous comment. "Remember there has been talk about this; are there now new reasons?"

"Yes," Niemeyer said, "the forthcoming April 18, when it will be 50 years that I started my academic career. I personally have nothing to request, no wish. God's grace and Your Majesty's favor have showered me with undeserved kindness. But the university, which wants to celebrate my jubilee, needs the gracious granting of the great kindness requested. Your Majesty's grace would give the celebration the right dignity and fill everybody with gratefulness and happiness."

The face of the King brightened, and, supporting his chin in his hand, he said thoughtfully and slowly, "So April 18th. Hearty congratulations and many happy years.—Well," he continued jokingly, "to cut a long story short, the question of pecunia. Also know a bit of Latin. One of my forefathers often used to say: non habeo pecuniam. A university building, if it is to fulfill its purposes, costs a lot of money—not easy to procure."

"But it would procure many blessings," Eylert put in, and then he added everything he could think of and had kept in his grateful heart for Halle, which had been dear to him all his life. But the King made no further comment. He ended the conversation rather suddenly and soon afterwards dismissed the party.

His valet Timm, who had faithfully stood by him and the queen on their flight from Napoleon via Schwedt and Küstrin to Memel, went ahead of him and led him to his study. The King dismissed him with a nod, went up to the window and looked outside.

His gaze went toward the Palace, then wandered to the left to the museum and the Guard House. How often had he stood here with Luise and looked at the old Packhof warehouse and the people on the street and envied them their limited, warm and cozy life, which he and his wife were not allowed to enjoy and that in those few days in Paretz at best found only a weak reflection.

Now Luise had been dead for seventeen years but still had her place in his heart. Three years ago, he had married the Countess of Harrach and had at the same time done everything not to diminish the memory of the dear deceased. At court the countess' rank was lower than that of all the princesses, but at least higher than that of the ladies of the city. He nevertheless thanked the Crown Prince for his insistence that the article in the "Document of Our Morganatic Marriage with the Countess Auguste von Harrach", which stated: "This relation is not to be regarded as a marriage of equals", be replaced by the milder sentence: "This relation is to be regarded as a morganatic marriage."

The Crown Prince had certainly had good reasons in that he didn't want to restrict possible daughters from this second marriage in their chances to get married, for which he as the next king would be responsible.

But children were not to be expected from this union. He had sought and found a merciful sister, a woman who loved him like a daughter loves her father, and no bedfellow, who all the same embodied what he liked, twenty-four years of age, thirty years younger than he, dark-haired, fresh and elegant. The summer house that Schinkel had built for him and his new wife in a cubic form in the Charlottenburg Palace park as an intentional contrast to the baroque palace was the right place for her to spend time.

He hadn't wanted a replication of Luise, never was that love to be replaced. But still he was glad to have the new partner. She had looked after him so devotedly and hadn't left him alone when he had broken a leg in the Palace at the beginning of the year. After he had recovered and shown himself to the Berliners at the window, people had sung in front of the Palace:

A victor's laurel crown for you
Your legs again are good as new.

They were both very amused. Outside it began to grow dark, the gas lanterns set up a year ago instead of oil lamps were lit. The streets, too, had been improved since the beginning of his rule. His valet at that time had told him in detail about his adventures as a pedestrian on the streets of Berlin and lamented the difficulties his wife had when she was on her way to the market. True, at first sight, the streets were wide and beautiful, but a pedestrian never knew how they were to protect themselves against the fast-moving coaches and wagons as well as against the mud and feces in the gutters. They were stopped constantly and had to jump over the gutters on to the so-called dam.

Nowhere could this inconvenience be better seen than on the Leipziger Strasse, allegedly one of the most beautiful in the whole of Berlin. When the weather was bad it was extremely muddy in the middle of the streets or on the dam, and there were countless potholes in the stone pavement, partly caused by the sandy soil and partly by the irresponsible neglect of the stone-layers and their foremen.

The large stones which were placed between smaller pebbles caused people to trip and fall to the ground. True, gutters ran along both sides of the dam, but in a way that caused them to form new and dangerous pitfalls. And chamber pots and kitchen waste were emptied into the gutters together with dead pets and other animals, which stank abominably. But as was often the case there were no funds available for road construction, then came the French, and only now things were picking up. At least shortly after he had become King street signs and house numbers had been installed so that orientation had become easier.

The King could just make out the shell of the museum, which was provisionally covered with a zinc roof. 700,000 thalers he had authorized and insisted that Schinkel make do with the money. He had also instituted a museum committee for the strict control of the finances and the construction and knew at the same time that Schinkel would have the decisive voice in that body, that is to say would take part in the decision about his own design and cost estimate.

Soon it had turned out that the authorized sum would be exceeded by 71,000 thalers, though based on reasonable grounds. Schinkel argued that the purchase of the plot, the buildings on the academy properties, compensation for the Flour House owned by the Bakers' Guild, and excavation work etc. had already cost about 140,000 thalers, so that only 560,000 thalers were left from the sum intended for the building proper. After presenting the very first museum memorandum only one year had passed when in early 1824 with the improving weather conditions the excavation of the building site and the shutting off of the Spree arm began. It turned out that due to the muddy and unstable ground the building had to be moved about 30 feet in an eastern direction toward the Stock Exchange, which he, the King, allowed under the condition that the building be brought into a straighter alignment with the trees that would surround it.

Schinkel had planned to erect the museum parallel to the Palace, which had meant a less advantageous position with regard to the surroundings. Sometimes, he thought, even he, the King, had to set his architect right.

To mollify Schinkel, he had granted his wish with respect to the great Granite Bowl.

"I humbly dare to submit to Your Majesty a devout request, the only reason for which is to benefit Your Majesty and the museum. It concerns the Great Granite Bowl for the museum. The most beautiful room of the museum, the Rotunda, for which the bowl was intended from the beginning provided it had a diameter of sixteen feet, would now, as the bowl has a diameter of 22 feet, be completely ruined in its architectural effect.

Also, the Rotunda would lose its original purpose, because the view of the classical statues between the columns would be largely obscured. Beside this important reason there is another which makes it desirable not to place the bowl within the building. The installation of such a large object of about one thousand six hundred hundredweight is a most dangerous operation, because it has to be transported into the building upright on its edge and only then laid down into its envisioned position. For this a tower-like scaffold of at least 60 pieces of lumber has to be erected, whose assembly and dismantling in that hall would not be possible without damage to the interior, which again would entail high costs. The smallest accident, for example the breaking of a pulley or the rupture of a rope could cause great harm to the building and the people working in it.

May I therefore most humbly beg to propose another place for the bowl. I believe that this colossal vessel should be placed in front of the great staircase in the Lustgarten, where it would embellish the location and the entrance to the building in a most desired way.

For explanation I allow myself to add a few view and perspective drawings for Your Majesty to look at and hopefully approve.

Your Majesty may believe that my humble desire is solely to serve Your Majesty and the common weal as best I can. Deeply devoted to Your Majesty,

Your most submissive Schinkel."

Quite alert, his Architect Superior and Privy Councilor. Without doubt he played upon the most important concerns of his lord, namely his frugality, therefore the reference to the additional costs, and secondly his reluctance to endanger human life, be it in peacetime or in war, therefore the reference to the dangers for the workers, should the bowl be taken into the museum.

The King, who, when he was alone, indulged all kinds of thoughts and feelings, which he normally had only revealed to Luise, not to other people, not even to his children, smiled to himself. He knew quite well that most of the people who surrounded him including those who wanted something from him, thought him a bit dumb, and not in the least like his great uncle, the great Frederick, whom he had met only with timidity and apprehension. And Frederick through his terrifying greatness had much contributed to his inhibition, his reluctance to talk freely in the presence of other people.

An over-eager servant had informed him about what Schadow had said about him and his father. He had said that the King loved his wife with his whole heart and that he also tried to rule in an orderly fashion and to the benefit of his country. But then he had said, "At the time of Fredrick William II, the present king's father, we had the greatest libertinism, everybody got drunk on champagne, ate the most expensive delicacies, and indulged in every lust. All Potsdam was a brothel, all families tried to find access to King and Court. Wives and daughters were offered like commodities, and the highest aristocrats were the most eager. Today it is hardly imaginable how pleasant is the example of our present King, the quiet homeliness, the beauty and decency of the queen. But basically, he is no likable master, and the queen had to endure much, and in this has shown her greatest loveliness. He is always dry, always sober, shy, terribly boring, and, worst of all, indecisive.

Jesus, how hesitant and vacillating he is, even the smallest matter needs to be thought over endlessly. His love for the queen, to be honest, was without real warmth and tenderness, and he didn't like the fuss made after her death, which caused him embarrassment."

They'd all be surprised if they knew how he saw through them and their intentions, even Schinkel, though he had to admit that he was faithful and on the whole obedient, and moreover had a beneficial influence on his eldest son, the Crown Prince. Baron vom Stein, in comparison, was an impertinent, disobedient and unwilling servant.

On the whole the King was at peace with himself with respect to the new museum building and the huge amount of money spent and the sum that was still to be provided.

In 1815, on the occasion of the Treaty of Paris, he had seen an exhibition of all the art treasures that Napoleon had collected and robbed from all over the world and had bought Giustinian's Collection. After their return to Berlin, the works abducted from Prussia were presented in an exhibition in the academy building Unter den Linden. The impression from Paris and the success of the exhibition in Berlin had induced him to commission the conversion of part of the academy to a museum according to modern principles.

In it the manifold art treasures that the kings of Prussia had collected were to be joined together, put into an instructive order, made accessible to everybody and also effective for the education of the nation.

After four years, in which the conversion of the academy stables overseen by Friedrich Rabe proceeded only slowly, the project so far financed out the royal privy purse was changed and from then on paid for by the state. An expert opinion found that the walls were damaged through corrosion by niter caused by the manure in the stables that had been housed on the ground floor for many years. In 1822, Schinkel was entrusted with the further conversion, and in the end the King was grateful that he had convinced him of the great advantages of a completely new building at the Lustgarten opposite the Palace. Beside the artistic benefits Schinkel had stressed the advantages gained from the modification of the waterways. But still the King had declined Schinkel's proposal to construct the interior columns from granite and insisted on the cheaper sandstone covered with plaster which looks like marble. Also, the doors had to be clad with bronze and the floor in the Rotunda made of marble slabs. More statues had to decorate the exterior.

On the other hand, he had not accepted the proposals of Professor Aloys Hirt, who wanted to replace the Rotunda by halls and passages because that would be cheaper.

The King, who knew that in matters of art and architecture he was not a trained authority, had Schinkel and the other members of the museum committee explain to him the aesthetic advantages of Schinkel's proposals. The hall at the front with eighteen massive ionic columns rising through two floors achieved the right proportional effect in relation to the Palace. And by having an open staircase to the upper floor a view into the depth was made possible.

Likewise, he had ordered his architect to be thrifty with money with respect to the design of the churches in the suburbs outside the city walls, Neues Voigtland, Wedding,

Gesundbrunnen and Moabit. He planned to finance them from his privy purse, after the collections in the Sophienkirche were unsuccessful. Modest churches without special adornment and spires were to be built. Altar furniture, candle holders and crucifixes should be cast from pewter. The building material was to be brick.

As usual Schinkel worked with abandon and had already submitted the blueprints. The King hoped that the churches would help to curb the immorality of the population in those places. He was deeply annoyed when he heard what kinds of amusement had come into use there. On the banks of the Spree river numerous public baths had arisen, and in pleasure ships called Lustkähne the Berliners visited the Moabit garden restaurants.

The police had reported to him how difficult it was to prevent lewd touching between men and women during these erotic trips. During the election of the senior journeymen organized by the Berlin women cooks there even happened such outrages that the Moabit police contingent of two officers had to be reinforced by a mounted policeman.

Another money-saving measure which he had insisted on concerned the theater, which had burnt down in 1817. Here he had ordered that the enclosing walls were to be left standing and reused for the new building. And lo! What a beautiful building had arisen like Phoenix from the ashes despite these alleged restrictions. Some gentlemen of his court, afraid to voice criticism, had looked at him as if he had insulted them. But Schinkel had been awarded the Order of the Red Eagle, Third Class, for his outstanding design.

Did people labor under the illusion that architects and artists could follow their fantasies and inspirations without any regard to the budget of the country? But whether he liked it or not, he would have to allocate the necessary funds for the new university building in Halle because, as the Crown Prince had told him, the continuation of the present untenable situation of such a famous university would reflect too badly on his rule.

How his gentlemen dragged and pulled him hither and thither, how they approached him with ever higher demands for money as if they didn't know that Prussia was a poor country.

This went so far that he had announced that all future construction projects had to be put under the strictest scrutiny. This meant the nonsense of keeping cost estimates intentionally low in order to make him agree to the envisaged project was to end. Either the responsible officials didn't know their business and couldn't produce realistic estimates or they hoped for additional funds when the building was already under construction. In the first case they weren't qualified for their positions, and in the second they deserved the appropriate punishment. That could entail the paying of the additional costs themselves.

Now they wanted to spend money lavishly, but when, years ago, he had warned against the raging enthusiasm that would inevitably lead to war against Napoleon, he was called a coward, of course behind his back. Nobody seemed to be aware of the ruinous costs and the inestimable suffering and death a war would mean. Even Schinkel, otherwise such a reasonable and sober man, entered the militia in the early summer of 1813, though despite all his patriotic enthusiasm he left it already in

August of the same year, maybe because he realized that when wounded or dead he couldn't design and build anymore and that he shouldn't sacrifice his creative talent on the battlefield. Others, less talented in architecture and painting were certainly more expendable and therefore well suited to fight against the arch enemy. He was right, and soon showed his ability when he put the King's draft of the Iron Cross into its final shape.

Others, the King was told, acted like bloodthirsty maniacs. The university professors formed a troop of their own and frequently exercised with their weapons, the small humpbacked Schleiermacher, who could barely carry the pike, on the very left, Savigny, tall as a lamppost, on the right wing, and Niebuhr, a lively dwarf, exercised so hard that his hands, normally holding the pen, got thick callus. The ideologically brave Fichte appeared armed to the teeth with two pistols stuck in his belt and dragging a heavy broadsword.

Schadow led the group of the artists, Iffland headed the heroes of the stage, those mostly in medieval or phantasmagoric costumes with weapons of the same vintage. Iffland himself carried the shield and breastplate of the Maid of Orleans, which caused great hilarity among the spectators.

Obviously, the disaster of 1806 at Jena and Auerstedt hadn't been enough of a warning. If ever a selfishness is forgivable then it is for a ruler who will keep peace for his subjects. When Napoleon, breaching the contract, marched through Ansbach and thus defeated the Austrians near Ulm, the war party including his brothers and Louis Ferdinand and even his Luise pressed for a break with France, for an alliance with Russia, for war. The talk was of the disgrace, that the honor of the Prussian

King was being trampled on, and people forgot that the biggest disgrace of man is war itself.

He could still see the uncomprehending and disconcerted look of his adjutant General Köckritz, when he said to him, "More than one king perished because he loved war, I will perish because I love peace." And this had almost happened.

He quite well remembered the campaign in France, in which he took part as Crown Prince.

The lack of care for the soldiers, the lowering of all moral standards in the war, the torments of the wounded, the many dead, all this he could not forget all his life.

The servant knocked on the door and came in after the King's permission. He lit the candles and asked for further orders. The King had none, dismissed him and sat on the fauteuil next to the fireplace. He wanted to be alone and remember the times with Luise, the times before he had to be king and could be happy as far as his nature allowed.

CHAPTER 5

I'm feeling hot and feverish, Susanne my love, put your cool hand on my forehead. It pains me that I failed to show you my love more, but God hadn't given me enough time.

The doctor gave Madame Schinkel a damp cloth, which she put on her husband's forehead. Then she administered a spoonful of broth to him, but while she was still bending over him, he again broke out into the agonizing and ominous cough they had witnessed earlier. Always when he was given something, particularly in liquid form, he choked, because the muscles needed for swallowing could no longer close the epiglottis properly. Then the cough sounding like whooping cough exploded from his chest, often alternating with a frighteningly noisy exhalation.

The doctor, who had tried to ease the cough by thrusting his arm under his back and lifting his upper body halfway, laid him gently down again. The cough had utterly sapped him. He lay with eyes closed, exhausted, breathing heavily.

Not God was the culprit, Karl. You wanted to build, for Prussia and its royal house, and, I think, for your own fame. You couldn't say no though you had drawn Thomas Telford's suspension bridge over the Menai Strait in Wales and written, my dearest Susanne, less is more. But in all honesty, for you less was not more, more it had to be all the time. You couldn't restrict yourself, you had to work untiringly, though in the end you were tired to death. You felt driven by a morbid sense of duty and the ambition of the artist. You have subjected yourself to the King when you couldn't go on as a free artist and our dear Gilly had prematurely died …

England, the new era, is making everything easy, doesn't believe in the world as it has long existed, lost the sense of its heritage and replaced it at any cost. The complete disregard for what has been created by our forefathers, this unrestricted belief in change makes people hurry on, leaving them no time to acknowledge things and enjoy them, which is a sure sign of the vanity of this era and of the people in charge.

People are so busy ensuring their existence that they don't have time for reflection but get lost in this frightening hustle. Oh, would people only recognize that not constant change, not the random but the existing as a result of manifold efforts are to be honored, because it represents something that is at nobody's disposal.

Wales, far and close at the same time, had received and accommodated us lovingly and taught us much. Like our beautiful Germany Wales is a strange friend among the peoples in Europe, and yet there is the desire to be there and become one with it.

After hesitating long, which was typical of him, His Majesty the King had authorized Schinkel's and Beuth's official trip to France and England in order for them to study museums and buildings in Paris and London for the benefit of the new museum in Berlin.

They had arrived at Dover on May the 24th, 1826, where they immediately enjoyed the view from the height of the castle.

They went as far as Scotland, and Schinkel could finally fulfill his long-standing desire to visit Fingal's Cave, also called Uamh-Binn, the Cave of Melody.

At four in the morning a sailor woke the whole party of travelers in the small place by means of dreadful bagpipes. The party was to sail to Staffa, an island about eight English miles off the west coast of Mull. They started at half past four. The whole time they had headwind and high waves; breakfast, as was usual, was taken on the ship, but due to the heavy seas Schinkel did not enjoy it.

The trip along the coastline became more and more gruesome and nightmarish, and intermittent rainstorms made the situation even more melancholic. Walls of highly weathered crumbling lava-like rock, in which basalt rudiments were visible, stood out from the higher mountains forming black caves with white seagulls fluttering around them. At times, however, the view was even picturesque. But Schinkel was unable to make sketches of any of it because, like others among the passengers, he got seasick.

They reached the open sea, where Staffa and other islands could be seen in the distance. While approaching Staffa, the daughter of the Scottish landowner in whose house on the Isle of Mull in Tobermory they had spent the night, gave them a rather learned talk about the island.

Staffa's highest point is about 138 ft above sea level, and the island is so small that one can walk around it in half an hour. Staffa derives from the Old Norse and means stave or pillar island. As with the other islands of the Inner Hebrides, Staffa belonged to the Crown of Norway until 1266.

The party applauded the young lady, who had so charmingly offered her explanations.

At 12 o'clock the island was reached and the travelers left the ship and walked up and down the steps formed by basalt columns while the wild sea foamed and roared about the lower parts in quite a frightening way.

They reached Fingal's Cave, which seemed like a church, very deep. The sea rose twelve to fifteen feet with every incoming wave, the thundering roar never stopping.

The Germans among the party sang in the background, and the cave, with its fifty-foot-high basalt columns standing like pipe organs, sounded like a big organ. The roof was a vaulted ceiling made of wild masses of rock. In the depth of the cave the sea looked green, and the whole black basalt rock appeared to the eye in a most beautiful purple.

After having admired this great natural spectacle sufficiently, all walked back along the dangerous paths on the broken off columns at the walls of the cave. Quite frequently two sailors had to hold a wooden stave as a kind of railing to protect the travelers from falling into the abyss. But just in case a small row boat with a number of sailors was kept ready on the wild waters.

Then all walked up to the upper level of the island on a small path along the rock face, which on both sides had steep chasms so that people had to be careful.

Some wild horses and a few cows, the only inhabitants of the island, raced away to the opposite shore when they saw people climbing from the depth. One couldn't help remembering Walter Scott's description in his novel "The Pirate".

Somebody had left a half-finished small stone cottage that was to serve as a kind of inn, whose walls now stood quite lonely on the bare surface.

The view from above to the many recesses and foreshores of the island, all of which were highly interesting with their caves and strange basalt formations, was very beautiful. Schinkel made a sketch of this wonderful world, then they climbed down on a more comfortable path into another gorge and wandered back to the steamboat over the small curiously formed basalt foothills.

Music caught his ear, The Hebrides, Fingal's Cave, where did it come from, was it just the echo of the sound of the sea in his ears?

How had the composer succeeded in avoiding a purely onomatopoeic approach, to which his visit of the Hebrides could easily have seduced him? No, his mastership had made him unite Ossian's Nordic motifs with his personal impressions of the Scottish sea and land and thus achieve a higher, transcendental musical image similar to William Turner's great painting, which the Royal Academy immediately included in its exhibition.

He made light and color, for which the objects deliver only vague points of reference, sole bearer of his paintings and reflect atmospheric moods and colors in a way nobody had dared so far.

How everything dissolves and loses its contours. And the continuation of the horizon into the sky can already be observed in Friedrich's works. This seemed to him to be threatening, the formless, rootless, non-committal, which at any time could lead to chaos.

Architecture, thank heavens, is of a very different nature, which forces the artist to keep order, to connect with the objects and make them the carriers of his ideas, admittedly in consideration of materials, gravity, purpose and surroundings.

This century will bring to the surface many new things, distances become shorter, since 1816 a steamboat called "Prinzessin Charlotte von Preußen" operates on the Spree and Havel rivers, the traditional laws of physics are already put in question by the artists in an anticipatory way, man doesn't know his place in society any longer. It confuses him if history isn't determined by reason, if no longer in every defeat, triumph, decline and every rise a general principle is symbolized that is higher than the previous one, just like in architecture. Architecture no doubt is the highest form of man's self-realization and thus a precondition of a life based on reason. Do people not want to understand that? In England the current architecture is the image of the new and questionable life, fleeting and partly ugly, achievements of engineering, artless, soulless, even though from time to time it produces impressionable works.

And his own soul, his nature, how did it find expression in his buildings? Has he not been ambitious and wanted to make the others build according to his gusto? Has he not impeded others in their development and careers by using his office? And has he not, tempted by his eagerness to do everything himself, to do everything better, made embarrassing mistakes?

He had not mastered acoustics as he should have, quite obvious in the Friedrichswerdersche Kirche and even more in the Nikolaikirche in Potsdam. After the inauguration ceremony of the former, that was in '31, the young preacher who had read the liturgy in front of the altar had lamented that it would be difficult to preach here due to the height of the church, worse, when the church was empty, the echo was too long. He, Schinkel, had been near enough to hear the criticism, but Zelter stood by him and said within the hearing of the young minister that it was quite new to him that sermons would be read in empty churches.

The acoustic problem in the Nikolaikirche was more troubling, indeed downright devastating. In addition to the annoyance that he was unable to get his dome design approved despite the Crown Prince's intercession with the King, the acoustics were very poor. That is, as he heard the King say after the inauguration in '37, better in an ordinary village church.

Vexed, the parishioners, who had entered the church with high devotional expectations, had not understood a word of the sermon when they left the church. Nor had they ever seen His Majesty more morose than on this occasion. "There we have now," said His Majesty, "the whole rich story. Outrageous! I have built the church with sympathy, I have examined, voted, compared, considered with experts, and I was pleased to fulfill the wishes of the citizens. I let it cost me a lot and never gave more gladly; with pleasure I looked out of my window at the building, I was assured that everything was good; it was wonderful. And now that everything has been completed, everything is spoiled, so that not a word has been understood.

Annoying! But it's not the first time that I am the dupe in an affair."

Schinkel was so depressed that the Crown Prince comforted him with the words: "Head high, Schinkel, we'll build together one day." He will not forget this of His Royal Highness.

The sick man became restless and moved his hands over the blanket as if searching. The nurse, who had been there for several days to give Madame Schinkel the opportunity to rest a little, approached his bed. He did not see her, but looked straight ahead, into the distance. The nurse spoke reassuringly to him, and after a while his hands became still.

He was praised as a great architect, and numberless honors had been awarded to him. His great plans and visions were admired, and the king was accused of restricting the great architect by his stinginess and stifling his creativity. But if he looked deep inside himself, he had to admit that his greatest and most lasting buildings were those where financial and other circumstances forced certain limitations on him, which on the other hand spurred him to high achievements. The exceptionality that the world constantly attributed to him was most evident in these constraints or even in the restrictions caused by political, economic and monarchical realities. He thought of the theater and the use the thrifty King made of the ruins, the enclosing walls. When it was opened with a prologue and Iphigenia on Tauris in the presence of the King, which Goethe had composed especially for the occasion, he was satisfied. The use of the enclosing walls of the previous building prompted him to design a three-part structure in which cubes of different storage and size interpenetrate. Everything else followed from this.

... After lunch they went on to Bangor, where they arrived in the evening. The inn in Bangor Ferry was situated in a lonely rural place between trees at the strait, called The Menai Strait, which separates the island of Anglesey from England. They immediately went to the big chain bridge which Thomas Telford had built and which had been opened at the beginning of this year—a work worthy of admiration. The chains are seven hundred feet long, the span is five hundred and sixty feet, and the bridge is suspended one hundred and twenty-one feet above low tide and one hundred feet above high tide.

They descended to the place where the chains are fixed in the rock. They go at least sixty steps deep into the earth. He recorded the situation in a drawing for his wife to show the immenseness of the object.

Beuth, committed to industry, was an unwavering adherent of the art of engineering and so together they could admire Telford's great work.

Forsooth, great are the achievements of the English industry, its masters and engineers, the enormous buildings, the factories, the tunnels, the steam engines for all kinds of purposes, the canals and roads, the mechanical workshops, the iron foundries and the gas works. The London Docks alone deserve admiration. The one thousand two hundred and sixty-two feet long, six hundred and twenty-nine feet wide and twenty-seven feet deep basin provides space for two hundred and fifty ships. Enormous magazines and vaults with stone stairways and double iron doors, railways for bringing in the goods and with iron cranes are all around. The wine cellars have room for twenty-two thousand barrels; above them are the two tobacco magazines, the largest of which is one hundred and sixty feet wide and seven hundred and sixty-two feet long. Enormous works of man, which, when Schinkel thought of their visit to Manchester, makes him wonder what it all boils down to.

In Manchester, the city's industry was in a serious crisis. Six hundred Irish workers from Manchester's factories had just been transported back to their homeland at the city's expense for lack of work, and twelve thousand workers came together for a meeting to start a revolt, for many of them, although they work sixteen hours a day, can only earn two shillings a week.

Much English military has now gathered in the city to keep order; the soldiers and officers are good to look at, and the horses on which they ride look magnificent.

The immense masses of the constructions, designed and overseen by a master mason without any help from architects and made of red brick just to satisfy the simplest need, create a most uncanny impression.

All this, in its contradiction of existence and transience, weighed heavily on his mind and made him think about the sense and purpose and, finally, the usefulness of architecture for mankind.

If we could extend ancient Greek architecture, holding on to its most spiritual principle, to the conditions of our new world, and fuse it at the same time with the best of all intermediate periods, then perhaps that would be the optimal way to solve the problems arising from the development of mankind and the humaneness that it requires.

On the return journey we traveled outside the stage-coach via Bath. The architecture of Bath is famous in England, but it is boring and completely dominated by the English trifles. The location of the city on hills and in valleys is pleasant and rich, but there is a lack of water surfaces and mountain lines of decisive character. Individual arms of the city stretch out in different streets arbitrarily into these hills and, although they are connected everywhere, a main plan for the whole city complex is missing. The Italian heat of the day was so intense that I soon had to return to York House, located on the corner of George Street and Broad Street, where I awaited Beuth, and then we had an excellent lunch.

York House was one of the relay inns for the stage-coaches, and its lunches enjoyed a good reputation. Schinkel and Beuth ate lamb with caper sauce and potatoes, then tried two slices of the popular bath chap, which consists of the lower part of a pork cheek wrapped around the pig's tongue and usually eaten cold. They drank ale with it, but both of them held back in view of the hot day. A Jewish woman from Berlin with her daughter, who came from Paris, entertained us a bit. Beuth engaged in a French conversation with her, and she was happy to be able to tell her story to her heart's content. She also took pains to display her Jewish superiority to the other guests.

Amused and at the same time frightened, we experienced a small scandal in which a drunken man smashed dishes and could hardly be put out onto the street by two sturdy waiters. The landlady apologized very much to her guests and said, "My house must not be desecrated; here sit two of the first gentlemen from Prussia, who honored me with their visit. What will these gentlemen think of England when they have to witness such things?"

They left the hotel for another walk through the town, turning right immediately and walking down the very steep Broad Street, from which they had a wonderful view of Bath Abbey in the middle distance and the tree-lined Beechen Cliff behind it.

As they walked, they observed the high terraces bricked up at the rear of the houses, which make up the streets toward the rise. In the streets, the patients visiting the local baths traveled in small three-wheeled carriages, pulled or pushed by a person, and equipped with a device by means of which the traveler could himself steer the chair in the direction he desired.

Schinkel was struck, as he remarked to Beuth, by the disgusting impudence and forwardness of the local public women even during the day. When he had made such remarks, Beuth said, "Can it be, dear friend, that you pay too little attention to the needs of the disadvantaged, the working classes and the poor and exploited?" Whereupon Schinkel said, "It may seem like it. But I believe that by my efforts to place architecture in the service of humanity, I am doing it a greater service than by a compassion that might help one individual here and there. Isn't improving man through art a more worthwhile goal?"

His friend retorted, "Our friendship and closeness allow me to say this. Take our visit to Edinburgh. You remember how, after lunch, we took a stroll around the castle to the old Grass Market, where a horse auction was held, and how you called the people in the taverns at that market riff-raff. Or take our visit to the flax mill in Leeds. You noticed that there were beautiful girls among the workers, but you did not notice the endless hours of work, the noise, the dust, the dirt, the absence of any possibility of at least brief recreation, the obvious signs of consumption on the red spotted faces of some of the workers, apart from the many technical details, or you did not comment on them to me, as you just commented on my conversation with the lady from Berlin, whose elegance you described as disgusting and Jewish."

Schinkel remained silent for a while and then said, overcoming his pride and slight offense at the criticism, "Beuth, dear friend, you may be right from your point of view. I don't like the hustle and bustle of the crowd; it repulses me and takes away my creativity. Pity for the disadvantaged makes me weak and pulls me away from my actual tasks. And concerning the Jewish woman from before, I feel the same as with the music of Meyerbeer, I don't like the pushiness that lies in both of them, just as I don't like the pushiness in anyone, Jew or Christian."

"Forgive me, Karl, do I detect a certain hauteur, which by the way, is quite at odds with your character, and a kind of bow to the spirit of the times, which you may have become acquainted with through Brentano in the Christian-German Table Society, to which, I remember, Philistines, Jews and Frenchmen were not admitted?"

"Perhaps," Schinkel replied, "it influenced me to a certain extent."

Beuth remained silent while they continued to follow one of the uphill roads. Then he said, "I don't quite understand how this influence can lead you to an attitude towards the Jews which can ultimately bring about a secession and demarcation that is to be rejected and to consequences that I do not even want to imagine." His tone had become somewhat sharper in this last moment, so that Schinkel said reassuringly, "In the end, my friend, Brentano and I were mainly criticizing the Jewish salons and the arrogance and contempt for the goyim that you can sometimes meet there."

Beuth remained silent for a while and then said, "Forgive me if I find this hard to believe. A just person like you must be measured by his humanistic standards. With such a generalizing condemnation as you used earlier, you are burdening a whole people with what you think you find in the unpleasantness of their individual representatives. If you do so, be just and generalize what incomparable things individual, not to say many, representatives of this people have achieved in the most diverse fields of artistic, scientific, industrial, technical, philosophical and commercial life from which mankind profits, and credit the whole people with it."

Schinkel clearly bothered, replied, "I understand what you are saying. But there is something in me, in my stomach, so to speak, that reacts with irritation to Jews, to their being chosen, their seclusion, their claim to the only God. Besides, Napoleon, who so humiliated our Prussia, emancipated the Jews, and this connection makes them additionally unpleasant for me."

"The same fallacy as before," Beuth said. "And as far as the only God is concerned, Muslims and Christians claim the same thing. Also, please don't forget that, especially after the overcoming of strict Eastern rabbinism, living in the Jewish way according to their own claim means living justly in the community and in the world."

Schinkel was unwilling to give in so quickly and reminded Beuth of Martin Luther and his opinion about the Jews and asked whether he, Schinkel, could then be completely wrong.

Beuth did not answer immediately, but seemed to fight down his resentment. Then he said, "May Luther, who pretended to preach the gospel of love, assuage his conscience of what he did to the Jews, no, especially the Germans, with his hateful and destructive outbursts. For his distorted interpretation of the Gospel, that Jews were under God's wrath and outside his grace, meant, viewed in the light of day, their exclusion from humanity, from the Christian community. Will he know what to say to God at the Last Judgment when he is asked, 'Doctor Martinus, and how have you treated my children, the Jews?'"

Beuth's voice grew louder and almost broke with despair, "By what right, I ask you, by what right is this done to our human brothers?"

He fell silent, breathing heavily, and Schinkel felt how difficult it was for his friend to regain his composure. He hoped, in the name of their friendship, that the displeasure would disappear the next day. Nevertheless, the thought of this did not leave him so quickly, and when he went to bed, after he had once more admired the night-chair, which, when closed, was purified by a stream of water and closed by a valve, he tried to discover what his opinion of the Jews in essentia was but came to no clear conclusion. He was displeased with Beuth's impudence at questioning his opinion of the Jews.

He decided to shelve the uncomfortable subject for the moment and began to think about how he would be able to use some of the inspiration he had received from English industrial construction and the use of cast iron for building and decoration.

The next morning found them in good spirits as they prepared to leave for London, although Beuth complained that his shirts had been badly damaged by a nail protruding from the floor of the coach during the journey to Bath. It had penetrated into his leather suitcase and his shirts. He had to have fresh shirts before arriving in Prussia and, since he had suffered the damage in the service of the King, they had to be paid for out of the official travel fund.

This helped Schinkel to regain his good mood. He took out the copy of His Majesty's Cabinet Order to the Minister of State and Finance von Motz dated March 21, 1826 and read it to Beuth.

"I have commissioned the Privy Chief Building Super-intendent Schinkel to travel to Paris and London and to gain precise knowledge of the establishment of the museums there, for the sake of the future establishment of a local museum. According to the present estimate, the cost of the journey is eighteen hundred thalers, and I therefore instruct you to transfer this sum to Privy Councilor Schinkel from the Extraordinario. Frederick William."

"And now, Beuth, dear friend," said Schinkel, "let us once again establish where we have been in a broad interpretation of the King's mission, albeit in the interest of the state, but also of ours. Paris, London, Brighton, Windsor, Edinburgh, Scotland,

Glasgow, Manchester, Liverpool, Wales, Bristol and Bath. I wonder if we could try to find another way to restore your shirts other than the travel fund?"

Beuth did not succeed in appearing determined. He finally smiled and said, "All right, let's try it. But you have to admit that this misfortune has befallen me in the King's service."

"Yes," Schinkel replied, "only the place of the misfortune cannot easily be brought into congruence with the travel route that the Minister of Finance would probably have considered the most favorable."

Then the journey took them back to London on the outside of the stage-coach.

CHAPTER 6

He seemed to feel the rocking of the carriage on the old road constructed by the Romans. They did not achieve much new in architecture, but their engineering structures were admirable and durable and, like this road, obviously lasted longer than a millennium and a half. They took particular care with the substructure. A firm stone foundation of coarse stones with a transverse layer was laid over the compressed ground. Several layers of smaller stones were then laid on top of this. Especially on the most important stretches, such as this one between Aquae Sulis, as they called Bath because of its hot springs, and Londinium, now London, the foundation was completed with a layer of large, six-inch-thick stone slabs, the summum dorsum, so that the total thickness of the road could be up to six feet. In addition, gutters were provided at the sides for drainage. The distance was indicated on milestones, which often bore the name of the emperor who had ordered the road to be built.

The carriage shook and swayed, it almost seemed as if he should fall to the floor when his wife and daughters lifted him out of the bed to change the sheet and duvet cover and wash him.

There was music again, no, not "Fingal's Cave" this time, but the Passion, Bach, Zelter, Mendelssohn, the memories came suddenly and clearly to his mind, how he walked with Beuth to the Sing-Akademie on the memorable 11th of March '29 to hear Bach's and Henrici's St. Matthews Passion. Unfortunately, his original design for the building was not accepted, but it was constructed on the site of the old moat behind the chestnut grove and the New Guardhouse, according to a version revised by Carl Theodor Ottmer. In '25 the foundation stone was laid, and Zelter—himself an expert in building and music alike—performed the ceremony.

Zelter had written in his foreword to the program booklet: "So this music, in two parts, between which the afternoon sermon took place, was already performed at the Good Friday Vespers in 1729 in the Thomaskirche in Leipzig, and celebrates its secular ceremony with today's repetition."

At first, Zelter, the old master mason, was not at all enthusiastic and had expressed himself accordingly when Mendelssohn came to him with plans to perform the Passion again. His experience had taught him prudence and renunciation, for it was already during Bach's lifetime that certain orthodox people had rejected parts of his music, including the oratorical Passions, on the grounds of alleged profanation of the biblical text or general incomprehensibility, as the following one-hundred-year-old anecdote testifies:

"When this Passion-Music with 12 violins, many oboes, bassoons and other instruments was first made in a noble city, many people were astonished and did not know what to make of it. In the prayer room of an aristocratic house there were many high ministri and noble ladies together, who sang the first passion song from their books with great devotion. When this theatrical music began, all these people were astonished, looked at each other and said: 'What is to become of this?' A noble widow said: 'God forbid, you children! It's like being in an opera comedy.' But all of them were heartily displeased with it and had just cause to complain."

Yes, they like nothing better than to complain, Schinkel thought and remembered what they had to say about the Schauspielhaus theater. Friedrich Weinbrenner, the simpleton, whose Düsseldorf theater design he had rejected in '20, called the theater a miserable architectural product, and wrote further: "Although H. Schenkel—he could not even spell his name properly—can be counted among the best draftsmen, he should not design a building project because it simply shows that he knows little or nothing about the true study of architecture."

The nagging reached as far as Weimar, so that Excellency Goethe felt compelled to request a report from his friend Zelter. There he sat, the friend, who reported to Weimar that the box offices were well placed so that nobody could slip by. He was pleased with the style of the whole thing, but the following gravamina were brought forward: The house was too small, the loges behind the balcony were too narrow, too dark, too low, even causing anxiety; the actors complained about their wardrobes and dressing rooms and so on. And the Berliners, always ready to mock, immediately had an answer ready as to why Schinkel was not present in person at the inauguration ceremony: There was not enough room left for the architect who had built the theater.

Schinkel was used to such condemnation. His intention had been to allow as many people as possible to hear and see well in as small a room as possible; these were the King's orders. As experience taught, one could hear and see well from all places. He refused to take seriously what the envy and the well-known censoriousness of the people otherwise brought forward as untenable, because it showed itself daily in different forms, depending on the mood. So, in the end, he was completely at ease with himself and did not allow resentment to dominate his life. His works were public, as were the musical works of Bach, and anyone could have their say.

Zelter, too, had not let himself be made crazy. Admittedly, in this more enlightened century the revival of the Passion was in the air, so to speak. Nevertheless, the young friends Eduard Devrient and Felix Mendelssohn Bartholdy, whose enthusiasm was not yet dampened by failures, had to work hard to reach their aim. They were successful by uniting what they were best at: Devrient's assertiveness coupled with diplomacy and Mendelssohn's brilliant musical talent. Yes, Schinkel readily admitted this to himself, one couldn't deny the latter this talent.

There was no lack of attraction from newspapers, and even if Schinkel did not like the baroque exuberance, he had to admit its effectiveness. The Berliner Allgemeine Musikalische Zeitung had announced a few weeks earlier:

"An important and happy event is about to take place in the musical world, but first of all in Berlin. In the first days of March, under the direction of Felix Mendelssohn Bartholdy, Johann Sebastian Bach's 'The Passion of our Lord Jesus Christ according to the Evangelist Matthew' will be performed. The greatest and most sacred work of the greatest composer will thus come alive after almost a hundred years of obscurity, a festival of religion and art."

The friends entered the great hall and looked around before trying to find their seats. Almost all the chairs were occupied;

all the big names of Berlin had come: The King and his retinue, then the outstanding names of Droysen, Hegel, Heine, Schleiermacher, Rahel Varnhagen and many others known to him. Schinkel recognized Rauch and Tieck and nodded to the two inseparable friends. He made a remark to Beuth about the illustriousness of the audience tonight and did not even notice how much he was a part of it.

Meanwhile Beuth had discovered their places. They sat down, not without some fuss, because Schinkel first had to take the drawing book and pencil out of his coat pocket. He immediately sank into thought, without bothering to listen to the babble of voices around him, in which individual words sometimes could be made out.

For the Greeks, music combined all the fine arts, was a gift of the muses and at the same time an invention of Pythagoras, which on the one hand means its adherence to the inspirational desires of music and on the other hand gives it a rational, mathematical foundation. This is probably the reason for the separation between musical practice and music theory, which has been more or less pronounced over the centuries.

Music, Schinkel thought, like architecture, is subject to the judgment of the crowd, before whose eyes and ears they both materialize. For their composition and execution both arts require certain unchangeable prerequisites that are inherent in man and dependent on physics, but within the limits of which they have great spiritual and material diversity. Today, music is mostly performed in closed spaces, as is the case tonight, and the architect must ensure that it finds the appropriate acoustic conditions, that is, conditions dependent on the design of the space.

Architecture, architectural, tectonic, tectonics, transformation of the architectural work into the art form, how all this unites architecture and music, when one says: In order to embellish, animate and explain, by virtue of an innate impulse, the architectural creation, which initially arose out of a naked need, in other words, to elevate it to a work of art, man transforms it, usually following the models contained in nature.

He prefers to take his inspiration from the plant kingdom, especially at an advanced level of culture, but he also draws on the other natural kingdoms. The simple, roughly hewn, elongated-parallelepipedic stone block would practically suffice to support the weight of the Greek temple complex. Artistically it was not enough for the Hellenes; they looked for models in nature to symbolize the functions that its support in the building organism should fulfill, and so they created the column with its parts. All healthy, exemplary building methods, including those of the Middle Ages, are based on such tectonic principles, notwithstanding apparent contradictions.

If one now, Schinkel thought, replaces building and stone and column and temple beams by musical-theoretical termini in these considerations, then one arrives at astonishing parallels. These are revealed above all in the ideas of harmony and disharmony, consonance and dissonance and their resolution, not to mention individual parts from which a musical work of art is constructed like a work of architecture. Didn't Master Goethe himself describe architecture as music turned to stone?

The oratorical Passion, which will be heard today, also has its own architecture with basic building blocks such as the texts of the Bible, Henrici's poetry, chorales and recitatives, which are put into relation to each other by Master Bach, thus creating a total work of art. Like the architect, the composer draws on what is already there, what has been worked on by others and then adds his own. And like a building, Bach's harmonies will remain and continue their impact on mankind.

The two choirs—here we have already what Bach distinguishes from others—are like builders in construction, they build the supporting pillars of the work.

While Schinkel thought and pondered thus, the choirs had lined up, about 150 singers, and the musicians had gathered. There was no organ available for the basso continuo, Mendelssohn himself would play the part on a fortepiano. The chorale "O Sacred head, sore wounded" with its wondrous verse

My days are few, or fail not,
With thine immortal power,
To hold me that I quail not
In death's most fearful hour:
That I may fight befriended,
And see in my last strife
To thee mine arms extended
Upon the Cross of life

should be sung by the choir without instrumental accompaniment. This song, Schinkel thought, is such a loving and understanding expression of the need for consolation of a person who is afraid of death, is so human that one wonders about other things by Bach.

Recently his chorale "By the Rivers of Babylon" was sung by a church choir in the Nikolaikirche as service music when Schinkel and his wife sought edification there, but admittedly he at the same time also wanted to find out about the structural condition of the building. Happily, with fresh voices, in a good mood and extremely intent on the uplift of the Christians gathered for the service of God, the Son of God and the Holy Spirit, the singers also served God with the last words of the 137th Psalm: "O daughter of Babylon who art to be destroyed; happy shall he be that rewardeth thee as thou hast served us, happy shall he be, that taketh and dasheth thy little ones against the stones."

This may have been the custom in earlier times, to kill the children by smashing their heads against rocks because they were future adult enemies. But how can one still today, in honor of God, express this desire, hardly pious, dressed in wonderful music, in the service?

How extremely imprisoned, thought Schinkel, shortly before the Passion began, is man in his time and little able to break through its limitations. But there are at least a few who are clear about this and rattle at its bars.

The keystone of the enormous and dramatic building of the Passion was the final chorus "We sit down with tears", sung by both choirs. Schinkel awoke from his reflection when the two choirs began. It is like the keystone of a cathedral, he thought, which means conclusion, support and coronation for the whole and completes it in the true sense of the word. As in architecture, repetition is used here and a motivic relationship to another building, no, a musical work, the St. John Passion, is established. But in the end the composer expresses a deep sadness by using a kind of disharmony unlike the harmonic function of the keystone in architecture.

The impression of the performance on the audience was great, and Schinkel and Beuth were also moved when they left the Sing-Akademie. The attendance at the following performances, which took place under Zelter's direction, since Mendelssohn had in the meantime begun a journey to England, did not dwindle, and in the following years it became a tradition of the Sing-Akademie to perform Bach's Passion regularly on Palm Sunday.

CHAPTER 7

"The state, Your Highness," Ancillon, tutor of the Crown Prince since 1810, wrote to him, "is not a Gothic temple in which one loses oneself dreamily. Because of your inclination towards constant drawing, even though you are very capable of it, I fear that the precious evenings would be completely lost, for I see you spending the whole time with a lead pen in your hand. For a future Schinkel this would be a very useful application, but because no nation has ever been ruled by romantic images, this eternal drawing will be a real waste of your valuable time."

The Crown Prince was, as so often, drawing when the valet brought the letter. The windows of his room in the palace were large and let in much light, the heavy curtains having been pulled aside. He had designed a "landscape" which excellently, he thought, expressed his romantic longing, mostly directed towards the south. The drawing, he found in all modesty, already contains an attempt that is more than the mere illustration of a course of events, it is the product of creative imagination.

It contains several villa-like buildings reminiscent of those of the two Gillys; in front of one there are stone benches and a terrace surrounded by a balustrade, before which one seems to descend to deeper terraces; next to it a little fountain pours into a stone basin; the background is a harbor bay overlooked by rocky mountains, a vision of the south, no doubt about it, nobody can deny him that.

No, he would in no way be dissuaded by this letter from drawing and designing, however much he began to appreciate his new teacher after he had to give up Delbrück with a heavy heart on the orders of his father. Delbrück, the Crown Prince was told as a reason for his departure, had influenced him in the spirit of the idealistic bourgeoisie and a sentimental, confessional religiosity with pedagogical principles, which the reformers deemed too soft, and possibly alienated him permanently from the principles by which the Prussian state was to be reformed.

Behind it was Baron vom Stein, who had leaned on the King, Stein, whose presence the King feared and whose insubordinate behavior made his hands tremble. The Baron prided himself on his equality with the Hohenzollern and did not consider himself their subject. He let the peace-loving and, as a consequence, often indecisive King feel this wherever he could. His intolerant self-righteousness and arrogant nature made him enemies even among his associates, who, like General Count York, called him a poisonous snake.

In the summer of 1808 Stein steered a dangerous course. In agreement with Gneisenau and Scharnhorst he supported the popular movement against the French that was developing all over Germany. The King rejected this movement as revolutionary and uncontrollable from the bottom of his heart, at least that is what he had told the Crown Prince. Stein eventually became the stumbling block, as Hardenberg called him when he committed the imprudence of sending a letter to Prince Wittgenstein, the Prussian Lord Chamberlain, discussing the idea of an uprising and the sources of money necessary for it. The letter was intercepted by the agents of Napoleon and published in the Moniteur. Stein was dismissed, and the King, under the influence of the Queen, made every effort to reappoint Hardenberg as State Chancellor, which he succeeded in doing after Altenstein resigned in 1810.

Stein, this hard-hearted man, did not let himself be softened even by the letter from the Crown Prince to the King, of which he was informed, but insisted on the dismissal of Delbrück, all the more so when he realized that the Queen, whom he accused of exuberance, lack of objectivity, impermanence, superficial education, tearfulness and what not, was in favor of Delbrück.

"Dearest, dearest father," the fourteen-year-old Crown Prince, who had fallen into a fever due to the threatened change of his teachers, wrote to his father, "if you love me and my most worthy Delbrück, if you wish me to get well again, do not separate me from him. I really cannot be happy without him."

The Privy Councilor in the Department of Culture and Professor of History Ancillon, who had a distinguished career in the service of the state ahead of him, had been an eyewitness to the French Revolution.

From this experience he had concluded that the preservation of the European system of states was the prerequisite for the existence of Prussia, emulating the admired Austrian State Chancellor Metternich. The enthusiastic Crown Prince, romanticizing the past, was very impressed by this attitude of his new educator; he followed him in most things even though he did not allow himself to be deprived of drawing and designing. And the fact that Ancillon brought Schinkel into the picture was, so to speak, a tactical error, for since Crown Prince

Fritz had recently met the master while looking at one of his dioramas, his admiration for the romantic painter knew no bounds.

Gropius and Schinkel, for lack of other means of earning money, had begun to produce perspective-optical paintings, panoramas and dioramas. The former were circular paintings, which can be viewed from their center and are both a realistic attraction and an illusion. Schinkel spent four months producing his "Panorama of Palermo" in oil, a painting more than 12 feet high and 100 feet long. From October 1808 he exhibited it near St. Hedwig's Cathedral in a specially built wooden rotunda, initially at his own expense.

After that, Wilhelm Ernst Gropius, the father of his younger friend, took over the presentation of the panorama, which had a considerable resonance among visitors, and assisted Schinkel in his efforts to become known to a wider audience.

Dioramas were even more popular with Berliners because they offered more room for illusion and imagination. In the most refined form of a diorama, a fabric that is as transparent as possible is painted on both sides with the same landscape, which appears on one side as in full daylight and on the other as at dusk or moonlight. This dual image is stretched onto a frame facing a window that can be closed by shutters and above which is another window whose light, with the help of a mirror, illuminates only the front of the painting. Once the viewer has observed this for a while, a screen moving silently on two rails is placed between the mirror and the painting, and at the same time the shutters which cover the lower window are opened, so that the painting is now viewed with light falling directly through it. By letting the light pass through colored glass, one can achieve a certain shade of color and can thus, for example, present the mornings and evenings or, like Schinkel, the fire of Moscow in 1812, to the lively "Oh's" and "Ah's" of the enthusiastic crowd. The basis of this showpiece was "The Twentieth Bulletin of the Great Army, Moskva", dated September 17th, 1812:

Moskva, one of the most beautiful and richest cities in the world, is no more. On the 14th the Russians set fire to the stock exchange, the bazaar and the hospital. On the 16th there was a violent wind; 3-4,000 wretches set fire to 500 places at the same time on the order of the governor Rostopshin. Most of the houses were composed of wood beams: the fire consumed them with incredible speed. It was a sea of fire. Almost everything was destroyed, though the Kremlin was saved. Several hundred murderous incendiaries were seized and shot.

The Berliners who had made it to the Mechanical Theater of Gropius at No 43, Französische Strasse, were rewarded with a fiery spectacle that inflamed every patriotic heart, because the retreat of the defeated French army through the Russian ice deserts was on everyone's lips.

The Royal Family, first and foremost the King and Queen, but also the Crown Prince and his brother Wilhelm, were great admirers of such dioramas and their half-dreamed up architecture, and it was on such an occasion that Schinkel became acquainted with the royal couple, which undoubtedly laid the foundation for his advancement in royal service.

The Crown Prince, too, had met Schinkel, his romantic master, so to speak, when he visited one of these paintings, and became his enthusiastic pupil from this time on. The acquaintanceship, which could almost be called friendship, also helped him to bear the death of his beloved mother, Queen Luise, who had deeply affected his youthful and sensitive mind. His mother had embodied his ideal image of a woman to such an extent that throughout his life women seemed to him to be something special, always mysterious and wise and at the same time pure and angelic. Even his later wife, the Bavarian princess Elisabeth, for whom he felt a deep affection in a childless marriage and to whom he wrote the most tender letters, could not compete with his mother.

Already in the seven-year-old's birthday letter, the great, natural, unconstrained love for his mother was expressed:

"Good morning, dear Mama,

I wish you happiness for your birthday and ask you to accept the drawing in the frame as a small gift. At the same time, I am sending you my copybook, and my and Wilhelm's drawing books, and I beg you to show all this to dear Papa.

Soon I will come and see you.

Berlin, March 10th, 1802"

"Hear my voice, my dear Fritz," she had written to him shortly before her death. "Consider what I tenderly repeat to you so often; tame the youthful fire with which you want to have everything you want, and for everything you immediately demand the means for its realization. Real freedom consists in doing what is good and what you recognize as such. Only by taming yourself will you come to the accomplishment of the good, and to have character means: after careful consideration of good or evil, to put into action what is recognized as the good, and to put all your willpower to it, so as not to let yourself be turned away by passions that might contradict the highest truth of the good."

Soon after she had written him the letter, she went to her home in Mecklenburg, to Hohenzieritz, where she died on July 19th, 1810, of general weakness caused by ten pregnancies, several illnesses and the strains of the flight from Napoleon.

The letter was dear to him, and the scent that rose from the beautiful, light yellow paper, the scent of his mother, the longing for her, and her irretrievable departure usually so numbed his senses that he had only a very uncertain idea of the meaning of the contents.

CHAPTER 8

"One cannot understand, Your Royal Highness, this enormous building, let alone maintain or even complete it, if one does not have as precise a knowledge as possible of its history, the construction process, of the masters involved and of the entire historical circumstances," Schinkel said to the Crown Prince, who was visiting him in his apartment on Unter den Linden. They wanted to come to an agreement on the necessary measures to preserve Cologne Cathedral.

It was a cold winter evening, the snow was a foot high on the streets of Berlin, and an icy haze was in the air. There were hardly any people left on the streets; whoever could, sat at home by the warm stove, if they had one. Every now and then a carriage passed the lime trees and shone its lantern fleetingly over the snow.

It was bright and warm in Schinkel's study. The large table under the windows was covered with paper, drawing materials, quills and sketches. At the opposite wall, on a small tea table, well-lit by a multi-armed candelabra, stood Caspar David Friedrich's painting "Monk by the Sea", which the King had bought at the Academy Exhibition in 1810 together with "Abbey in the Oakwood" and donated to the Crown Prince. The King loved this atmosphere of mist, yearning sadness and Gothic.

For Schinkel at that time, "Monk by the Sea" was a completely new kind of painting, in which landscape was understood as reaching far beyond the horizon depicted.

"To the magnificent view over the sea," Schinkel had read in the article "Emotions in Front of Friedrich's Seascape" in the "Berliner Abendblätter" of October 13th, 1810, "belongs without doubt that one should have gone there, that one must go back, that one wants to cross over, that one cannot do so, that one misses everything in life, and yet one hears the voice of life in the roar of the flood, in the blowing in the air, in the drifting clouds and the lonely cry of the birds. No situation in the world could be more sad and eerie than this, as the only spark of life in the wide realm of death is the monk, a lonely center in a lonely circle. This definitively marked a complete new stage in Friedrich's art since in its uniformity and boundlessness it has no foreground except the frame; it is as if one's eyelids had been cut away."

Brentano had submitted the article to the chief editor, Heinrich von Kleist, who, to Brentano's annoyance, had almost completely rewritten it because he found it was too pompous.

After he had viewed this painting, Schinkel had sensed, reinforced by Kleist's and Brentano's description, that, however much he had developed as a painter and was praised by the people, he would not achieve such greatness in this art. This had not upset him, but rather strengthened his conviction that his true destiny was architecture. Incidentally, he remembered, without losing any of his admiration for the painter, that Excellency von Goethe hated the mixture of melancholy and longing for death in Friedrich's and other romantic painters' works.

For this evening, the Crown Prince had brought "Monk by the Sea" with him in his carriage so that they could view it together at leisure and had had it transported to Schinkel's apartment by his servant, because he knew how much his father's master builder and his, the Crown Prince's teacher would enjoy it.

After they had both looked at the picture for some time, Schinkel said, "Your Royal Highness knows that I want to see traces of man in the landscape, in nature, preferably through architecture. I then feel as if man's beneficial rule over nature is expressed, as if both the destiny of man and of nature is made obvious. There should be a fruitful interrelation dominated by man's creative spirit but taking into consideration at the same time the characteristics of nature. A landscape in which no human element is present can be great and beautiful, but the beholder becomes vague, restless and sad because he would like to find out how his peers have taken possession of nature, lived in it and enjoyed its beauty."

To this the Prince responded, "Well, my dear Schinkel, we won't find much of that in this picture. But nevertheless, there is a human being here, perhaps as a part of nature or as a humble observer and as someone who, with a yearning and restless soul, is trying to recapture the long-departed oneness."

Thereupon they had sat down at the warm tile stove on two comfortable wooden chairs with backrests and cushions. Before that, there had been a light dinner in the living room, prepared by Susanne Schinkel's mother, a potato dish with ham. Susanne's mother had been living with them for some time, to assist her daughter, especially during the time when she was pregnant with Elisabeth, called "das Lieschen". Afterwards they had had tea, which was now on a small side table next to Schinkel.

On the one hand, Schinkel welcomed the visit of the Crown Prince, because he appreciated him as a patron of his projects and an understanding art lover, though often lost in romantic visions, who had already achieved a great deal with the King. On the other hand, however, the visit cost him time, which he urgently needed for his work, which he no longer accomplished so easily. Lately he had been feeling worn out and even ill and had often to use cures. But he forbade himself any impatience during such a visit; rather, like his visitor, he had crayon and paper at hand, ready to illustrate his words by drawing, which was his habit.

"You are absolutely right, dear Schinkel," said the Crown Prince now, thus resuming the original theme, "and that is why I have, thoroughly I hope, studied the cathedral in preparation for our conversation. I have been interested in this magnificent building ever since I visited it on my return from the French Campaign with Messrs. Boisserée, Ancillon and General Knesebeck, and we climbed the weathered walls at the risk of our lives and without heeding Ancillon's warnings. From the Dragon's Gate we walked around the whole building to the main entrance. From there we went to the glass paintings in the nave, then to the choir, from there to the sarcophagi of the three kings and finally out onto the roof. The well-fed gentlemen of my company gasped and sweated, but they didn't really complain, for the building had exerted its magic on them too, and finally they had to admit that after seeing all the great works in France, this one deserved the crown.

As the future sovereign, should it not offend me that in the history of Cologne Cathedral to this day there has been no, or almost no, royal or imperial authority at all? That will change. If our plan is successful, our names will be inextricably linked to the restored and completed work of art, just as the current building will be linked to the name of the master builder Gerhard von Rile, about whom we unfortunately know hardly anything. He was certainly present, however, when the Archbishop of Cologne, Konrad von Hochstaden, laid the foundation stone for a church in 1248, with which the citizens of the great city wanted to establish an appropriate pilgrimage site for the relics of the Three Magi.

Rile then not only managed the construction during the first twenty years, but also delivered the overall plan of the building, which, my dear Schinkel, we want to complete as the German National Cathedral. For such a National Cathedral is like a king, powerful and domineering and sovereign, to whom Christianity looks up in faith and obedience, and before whose face every libertarian thought is abandoned. It will be as it was in the past, when everyone knew his place and his value and fulfilled it righteously and faithfully."

The Crown Prince paused, took a sip of tea and looked expectantly at Schinkel, thrilled by his own words.

Schinkel did not at all share his counterpart's opinion of the symbolic and metaphorical value of a restored Cologne Cathedral. He therefore decided to respond in a way that did not dampen his royal pupil's enthusiasm more than necessary, while at the same time not betraying his own ideas too much. As learned earlier, a theoretical approach helped in this respect.

"The high opinion," he said therefore, "that Your Royal Highness has of your future profession can't be praised enough. My work, however, is that of a builder, which is naturally different from the high task that awaits Your Highness. The art of building is a unity, whether it be new construction or restoration. I consider architecture and its results, the buildings, as the continuation of nature in its constructive activity."

"Hold on, Schinkel," the Crown Prince interrupted him, "how is this to be understood, continuation of the constructive activity of nature?"

"Well", Schinkel replied, "nature and everything it produces is without question subject to the same physical laws as everything created by human hands. And nature, of which we are a part, has endowed us with a feeling for beauty, for harmony of colors and tones, for symmetry and thus also for the beauty of asymmetry and dissonance resolving itself. All of this is inextricably linked, though not always directly, with the practicality that is an indispensable feature of nature. And from this we develop the laws of aesthetics. As Your Highness can see, this results in what I call the continuation of natural creations."

"Shall your words mean," asked the Crown Prince, "that nature has endowed us with a sense of beauty, that every human being is endowed with such a sense and artistic talent, the latter therefore not reserved for a few chosen ones?"

"Certainly, Your Royal Highness, this is what I believe. In many it's only buried by circumstance and the vicissitudes of time. But if, in continuation of nature's activity, we build aesthetically, making people aware of what is beautiful, returning to the essentials of what nature has prescribed, or should I rather say concentrating them as with a burning- glass, then we help to dig up the buried artistic talent and contribute to the higher development of mankind."

The Crown Prince had listened to Schinkel's last words with growing restlessness. Then he said, "Don't you go too far here, dear friend, by making all people equal, and thus bring an egalitarian spirit into our conversation that I cannot share at all, and which I will rigorously fight against, should I ever have the chance?"

Schinkel became slightly discouraged because he had carelessly caused the Crown Prince to become uneasy and maybe to draw conclusions about his, Schinkel's, views, which he had not intended to reveal so clearly. But for himself he had to come to these views because he wanted to be consistent. Architecture is a public event and therefore subject to the judgment of the crowd. And the judgment of the crowd must be trained so that they are able to judge correctly, which would require a certain level of emancipation, a certain transcending of class boundaries, as Schinkel had seen it in England in its early stages. It was obvious that the Crown Prince could not approve of that.

At that moment the door opened and Madame Schinkel stepped inside. She carried a tray with both hands, on which there were a plate of biscuits and two glasses of red wine.

The Crown Prince turned to her and, while she was placing the tray on the small table, said, "Help me, my dear lady, to take our Schinkel away from his French thoughts. Just think, now he believes all men are equal. This is not far from declaring them all equal by nature."

Susanne Schinkel looked at her husband lovingly and caringly and said, "Your Highness must not take this too literally. He has always buried himself in his work, no longer even looking up, and thus cannot see that the circumstances do not conform to his thoughts. The art of building is his life and possibly leads him to generalize its laws too rashly and apply them to humanity."

She placed the tea set on her tray, performed a curtsy, went out and left two very astonished gentlemen.

CHAPTER 9

"You have a devilishly clever wife, dear friend," the Crown Prince said to Schinkel, who smiled and said, "She is clever, but whether she is right with this remark, I'm not sure. Let me also say, Your Highness, that true architecture is always preceded by the creative idea, for the realization of which it is imperative that this idea be established following the general laws of reason. The practical implementation, however, must be left to genius."

The Crown Prince laughed. "Is this what you think when I give you the notes with my building ideas and say, now make something out of the scribblings? The latter would then be the creative idea that precedes the architecture, which I then rightly leave to your genius to realize."

Schinkel replied, "What I said, Your Royal Highness, is the ideal. In reality, His Majesty's purse, the specifications of location and material, as well as the limitations of my own mind determine what is finally constructed. Nevertheless, we must not lose sight of the fact that the art of building, which is a unity of craft and science, is determined by scientific progress and changing living conditions. The task of improving the living conditions of the people in every sphere of life is the noblest task of the sovereign, and here Your Highness will certainly agree."

He took one of the glasses of red wine from the tray and held it out to the Crown Prince, who took it and said, "Yes, I think here we are of the same mind. To your health, Schinkel." They tasted, drank and praised the wine.

Then the Crown Prince continued, "But now back to Cologne Cathedral in connection with the thoughts you have just expressed. How does that fit together?"

Schinkel took a biscuit from the plate and ate it. He then drank a sip of wine, which gave him time to get his thoughts in order.

"To explain this connection, I must go back a little. The oldest Egyptian and Greek works were often built with an immense effort of physical force, which expressed the idea of greatness and imperishability of earthly power. With the progress of science and its application to art, the free power of the spirit over the material world reduced the expenditure of physical force for the construction of a building. With science progressing, I repeat, based on the art education of the Greeks, the construction of vaults came into being and reached its highest form in the Middle Ages. This meant a further step in the predominance of the spirit over an infinite new field of matter.

And now we come to Cologne Cathedral, the importance of which, with all due respect to Your Royal Highness's opinion, I note particularly here, because the same freedom of the spirit, elevated by Christianity, is found in the construction of the medieval churches, where the idea of sublimity and the reality of striving for height merge completely. Thus, the physical construction makes visible that we humans are directly connected with the supernatural, with God, which can be taken literally or as an image for man's godlike dominion over matter."

The Crown Prince's mouth had opened when he listened to this explanation. He closed it hastily when Schinkel had ended.

At that moment, Madame Schinkel came in and said, "Your servant is waiting in the hall, Your Royal Highness."

"Please send him in," replied the Crown Prince. The servant came in and Schinkel gave him the painting by Friedrich, which he carefully wrapped in a cloth he had brought with him.

"As much as I would like, I can't leave you the picture," said the Crown Prince when Schinkel regretfully saw the painting disappear under its wrapping. "And what measures we have to take next regarding Cologne Cathedral is reserved for another conversation."

He thanked Madame Schinkel for the hospitality, said goodbye to her and, accompanied by Schinkel and following the servant, went down the stairs to the street and to the carriage. He got in and said goodbye. "Thank you, dear Schinkel, for the good talk. One never leaves you without intellectual and artistic gain." With this he gave a sign to the coachman, who waved the whip over the horses, shouted "Hi!" and the horses, which were emitting white steam from their nostrils in the cold, set off.

Schinkel stayed for a short while outside in spite of the cold and looked on as the coach moved off. If you are to be king one day, he thought, your inclination towards the Middle Ages and my views will probably be more and more at odds when we work together on construction projects. You are repeating what has been, whereas I believe that nothing completed in history should be repeated because otherwise history is not newly created but brought to a standstill. No, we must create something new which is capable of allowing history to continue, to progress, to go forward.

He took another look in the direction of the palace towards which the carriage had gone and went into the house. He wanted to study the drafts of Sulpice Boisserée and then make a proposal about the steps to be taken for the preservation and, hopefully, the completion of the cathedral.

In his coach the Crown Prince smiled silently to himself. His Schinkel was an extraordinary man, without doubt, a man of principle and genius. And what he had already achieved for his country and its reputation was tremendous. The Royal House had every reason to be satisfied and also grateful to have won such a servant. And yet he was only human, which the Crown Prince had not wanted to believe when he was younger, when he treasured him above all others as a painter and architect.

He certainly had expressed his noble principles of architecture and restoration, had the Porta Nigra in Trier repaired after his return from the Rhineland, had taken care of the preservation of the gate building of the Royal Bank, the restoration of the sculptures on the roof of the Zeughaus arsenal, the preservation of the statues on the Royal Guesthouse at the Werdersche Markt, the renovation of the Nicolaikirche and much more. And yet he had more or less betrayed his own principles for dealing with the testimonies of the past when he wanted to provide the church in the city of Stralau with a tower in the classical style where the simple design by Langerhans proved to be far more appropriate. The Church of St. Mary— late Gothic—in Frankfurt on the Oder river, for example, he had provided with Corinthian capitals in the interior, just think of it. And how had he changed Brandenburg Cathedral during the renovation work. And didn't he consider demolishing the pharmacy wing with the beautiful gables here at the Palace because he needed space for a monument to the great Friedrich? Called the pharmacy an unsightly building in his "Architectural Designs", cleverly avoiding the word demolition, but wrote, "Design for a monument to Frederick the Great on the site of the old court pharmacy in Berlin".

Oh, my dear Schinkel, you wanted to sacrifice the old academy building for your department store on Unter den Linden, you also suggested that the old library building of Fischer von Erlach be removed completely and that a more appropriate building for the Royal Library be constructed.

I believe, thought the Crown Prince, that behind this was your aversion to the baroque. Did you not write in a letter from Silesia, "The baroque style of the church is a sign of the deepest decline the architectural taste has ever suffered in Europe."

The Crown Prince shook his head in his carriage about these inconsistencies, which, on the other hand, because they were so human, brought the master builder closer to him.

In front of the Palace the carriage pulled up, the servant jumped down from his seat, opened the door for his master and let down the little stairs. The Crown Prince alighted and went into the Palace where he had a residence on the first floor, completely furnished by Schinkel. He hurried to his chambers as he felt the urge to tell his wife about his latest thoughts and his talk with his tutor.

In the City Palace Schinkel had also furnished living quarters for the King, and for the princes Karl, Albrecht and Wilhelm he had taken over the interior design of their palaces. And the King's uncle, Prince August, a nephew of the great Frederick, head of the Prussian artillery, had sent an order to Berlin just four days after the invasion of Paris that he wished to have lounges on the upper floor of the palace at 65 Wilhelmstrasse, for which he provisionally ordered silk fabric. Schinkel was to be consulted because he had the right taste in such matters.

But Schinkel had to decline, saying he didn't have the time to satisfy the wishes of His Royal Highness this winter. He was busy with a large number of private commissions from His Majesty the King and Chancellor Hardenberg. The King and Prince Hardenberg were at the Congress of Vienna, and he had to use their absence for the conversion and furnishing of their apartments.

It was only after the Battle of Waterloo that he was able to begin work on the Palace of Prince August, successfully recommending his brother-in-law Berger as a construction contractor. For silk supplier, Schinkel called on his friend Gabain, who, at his suggestion, supplied the fabrics without patterns so that the ornaments could be embroidered on them according to the shape of the furniture.

In his conscientiousness, Schinkel even supplied the various color mixtures of the stucco marble on a strip of paper as a model for the workers. He not only provided the designs, but also had to supervise the work of the craftsmen. He negotiated with the suppliers about the value of the timber, the quality of the fabrics, the prices and delivery dates. He drew up contracts and checked the invoices.

In July '16 he had to hand over the construction supervision to his brother-in-law Berger as he had received the order from Bülow and Hardenberg to travel to Heidelberg. After his return, it took another half year until the last furniture for the palace was delivered, the four large chandeliers for 28 candles and the gold-plated door handles with rosettes—all according to his drawings. At the inauguration there was a dinner and a big ball with 250 guests, and Schinkel received a bonus of 1,000 thalers, with which the prince expressed his utmost satisfaction.

CHAPTER 10

Father, dear father, you set me on my way before you left us so early when you died after helping to extinguish the great fire in Neuruppin, which consumed the whole town and hurt you so lethally.

Now I am lying here, burnt out as well and with aching wounds, and you cannot help me. The little birds you drew for me were lovely, and yet the little boy, just six years old, said, "A bird looks very different, Papa. Thus, for example ..."

The adjutant, whom the King had sent to check on the sick man and report on his condition, turned to the family doctor in surprise, "What does this gesture of the hand of our dear patient mean? Does he do it often?"

Dr. Pätsch answered, "His mind doesn't seem to work any longer, but I can't really believe it. With the rest of his will he delves into his memories and recalls things, completely broken and incoherent, sometimes more clearly, sometimes more confused. I interpret this hand movement as him trying to draw something. And sometimes he utters infantile sounds that could make you believe he is back in his childhood."

"That is certainly not unusual," said the adjutant wisely, "because as we grow older or when our powers of thought diminish, we remember more clearly things that have long since passed than things that are more recent."

The doctor, who felt that this remark was an amateurish pronouncement on his competence, approached the sick person to avoid a reply and felt the architect's pulse.

Schinkel sensed the slight pressure of the doctor's fingers on his wrist and struggled to say something.

"His thoughts are in Neuruppin, in his childhood," said Susanne Schinkel, who had just stepped in, surprising the two gentlemen. "The lively movements and expressions are a faint reflection of his childhood and of what he was like back then. His sister Charlotte, head of St. Katharinenkloster in Stendal, had told me that his character very early took on certain distinct features, he showed himself to be modest, reserved, comfortable, but also quick-tempered and inclined to anger. Schinkel's mother, a born Rose and close relative of the famous scholarly family of the same name, to which the chemists and mineralogists Valentin, Heinrich and Gustav Rose belonged, moved to the Pfarrwitwenhaus after her husband's death. This was spared from the fire at the time and has been preserved until today. The town, by the way, was rebuilt beautifully by the blessed grandfather of our King after the fire of 1787.

In this preachers' widows' house, with the old pear tree in the yard and an old-fashioned garden behind it, my dear husband spent his boyhood, from the age of six to fourteen.

Karl was not excellent at school, perhaps because every kind of artistic exercise captivated him from an early age, and a more intimate relationship with books was not possible. His musical talent has always been great; after listening to an opera, for example, he reproduced it on the piano almost from beginning to end. Theater was his main passion from early on. His elder sister wrote the plays, he painted the characters and cut them out. And in the evenings, he'd put on a puppet show."

"Go ahead, Madame. Perhaps we'll find something in his early life story that will give us a clue to his illness and how to treat it."

"I don't think that's very likely," replied Madame Schinkel. "The family moved to Berlin when he was fourteen years old, and he only came to Ruppin on a visiting basis, especially to Kränzlin, a nearby village whose pastor his elder sister married. Since you are asking me about certain causes, it now strikes me how many generations of the Schinkels—three I think—were exclusively churchmen. And almost all the women married preachers in the Mark Brandenburg. Karl was the first male descendant to take up a secular profession after the said three generations."

"How, Madame, can this fact be a cause of illness?" asked the doctor.

"I don't really know," replied Madame Schinkel, "but this eternal compulsion to always be more moral than others in public because he descended from a pastor, and then to be the only one in the class, even in the whole school, as a child of a pastor ..." She stopped here because she didn't know how to go on.

The adjutant stepped in, "Isn't it almost like the royal children whose unique position also means a lot of pressure?"

Here the doctor saw a suitable opportunity to put the adjutant in his place. "I don't think we can equate this so easily," he said. "The parson's child, although often uncommon in school and class, lives nevertheless in the ordinary world and has to make friends with it, while the royal child remains in another world all their life and is therefore not subject to such tensions."

He turned to Madame Schinkel again and said: "Now I understand what Madame means. On the one hand we have the moral claim which the pastor-father raises loudly by virtue of his office, daily or at least on Sundays luring with heaven and threatening with hell, and on the other hand the boy with his human weaknesses and the constant scrutiny by the surrounding world, which makes life difficult for him with their constant 'You of all people as a pastor's son ...'. That must almost force you to dissimulate and to be hypocritical if you want to survive.

Whoever gets through it must be of very strong character and lays early the seeds of future overwork, which is his way of responding to the challenges of the world, of always having to be better, more diligent, more honest, more Christian than the others."

"Yes," Madame Schinkel interjected, "that's exactly what Karl once said. And if, he added at the time, the parson's child has no talent—which I had, thank God—they easily tend towards the life of a dilettante, moving between arrogance and servility."

"I can summarize all of this, although it does not help us in the treatment of the patient, by saying that Schinkel suffers the consequences of a lifelong overexertion caused by his continuous activity and artistic production. This uninterrupted restlessness may well be the result of the described unique position as the son of a pastor as well as the Protestant upbringing associated with a Prussian duty ethos."

Madame Schinkel, who had listened very attentively, said, "Karl once told me that the obligation to continue the unfinished private buildings of Friedrich Gilly, his revered teacher, after his early death created a certain restless activity in him from a very early age, which he later, because it had become a kind of second nature to him, couldn't give up. But I must not forget, he said, that he also owed a great deal to this difficult heritage. He added that the insurmountable inclination of his imagination, which he fought against incessantly, but which nevertheless always drove him to work in an almost pathological way, made things even harder. It sometimes seemed to him that his mind ruled his body in a cruel way."

She approached her husband's bed and looked at his face for a long time. Dear husband, she thought, you have been the happiness of my life. When you were courting me, and my father finally agreed, we had to wait another two years for the wedding because of his bankruptcy during the French occupation, until we were married in the Stettin Jacobikirche and then drove to Frauendorf on the Oder river for the cheerful wedding ceremony.

Last weekend I was there again with Elisabeth after a long time. I can never enter that place without remembering that day and every hour of it with increasing love. You led me to the fountain where our faces were reflected. This well, my dearest Susanne Eleonore Henriette Schinkel, née Berger, will still keep our reflection when we are long gone.

Remembering these words of her husband, she could not hold back her tears. Deterring the doctor who wanted to comfort her, she went outside and cried bitterly.

CHAPTER 11

Christian Daniel Rauch and his friend Christian Friedrich Tieck visited their friend, the painter, architect and town planner, the Head of the Oberbaudeputation Karl Friedrich Schinkel.

It was a beautiful early summer day, the lime trees were in blossom and their overwhelming scent was everywhere, wafting through the open windows of Schinkel's study and sickroom on the second floor of the Allgemeine Bauschule, generally called Building Academy. It housed two Royal Prussian institutions, the General Building School or Bau-Schule under the direction of Peter Christian Wilhelm Beuth and the Oberbaudeputation, the Royal Office of Public Works. The auditoria and drawing rooms of the Building School as well as the library and collections were housed on the first floor of the four-story building. The second floor contained, in addition to the director's residence, the rooms for meetings, the registries and the other necessary rooms of the Oberbaudeputation. The top floor was used for storing files, the ground floor was reserved for twelve shops.

The friends were asked by the maid to wait a moment in the vestibule of Schinkel's apartment as the patient needed to be prepared for the visit. They spent their time waiting by looking at the pictures hanging on the walls, which they had known for a long time and which were mostly works by Schinkel himself.

After a while Susanne Schinkel came in and welcomed them. Tieck gave her a bottle of wine and Rauch a bouquet of tulips. She handed both to the maid telling her to put the flowers in a vase and to supply them with water. Then she asked the visitors to follow her. They passed through the living room, where engravings by Raphael were hanging, then through a room painted reddish brown, where on a shelf were plaster casts of antiques, on special pedestals the Juno Ludovisi, the Zeus from the Vatican Museum and The Praying Boy.

Normally, said Susanne, a door from the vestibule leads directly into the anteroom of the study, but due to the circumstances of her husband's sickness she felt compelled to ask her friends for this little detour. In the anteroom in question, all kinds of utensils had to be stored that were connected with Schinkel's bedridden condition.

They went into the study where the sick man was lying in his bed, which stood with the foot end facing the open window so that he could look out.

Rauch and Tieck approached the bed from both sides and greeted their friend with hushed voices, but he did not react at all, except with a certain restlessness of his hands, and instead turned his eyes towards the window. His wife had combed back his silver-grey hair, shaved him and dressed him in fresh nightwear. His face was pale, his eyes gazeless, his lips bitten and partly covered with a crust of blood. He breathed shallowly and quickly, but fairly regularly.

The two visitors were not surprised by the lack of reaction, as they were aware of the condition of their friend. After gently stroking his restless hands, they stepped to the window and looked out. They saw the bridge that Schinkel had built, their gaze went to his museum, which, together with the cathedral he had redesigned formed the square space he had created. On the opposite side of the house they knew was the Friedrichswerdersche Kirche, not far from it the Schauspielhaus theater. And within the larger vicinity there were witnesses of further activities everywhere: administrative buildings, warehouses, monuments, residential buildings, palaces and churches.

This life's work of their friend, which lay before them and which extended far beyond Berlin and Prussia to wider Germany and even to distant lands, was unparalleled.

In addition, the pictures he had painted hung in many buildings, the furniture and furnishings he had designed, such as chairs, bureaus, cupboards, chandeliers, and his wall decorations, interior furnishings, stairs, stage sets, vases, and candelabras, were on show in many places.

His writings, which dealt with the questions, problems and the nature of architecture, could be read in the libraries; his calculations, reports, requests, letters, entries, drafts, cost estimates, reminders, proposals and drawings in the offices and chancelleries.

And they themselves now were in the Bauakademie or Academy of Architecture, a work which, and this was something they had often talked about this year when their friend was already bed-ridden, pointed far into the future of architecture with its combination of functionality and beauty.

The freestanding building rose on a square ground-plan with an inner courtyard; its facades, which were strictly symmetrical in themselves, were identical. The building was made of brick without whitewashing or plastering, which, as Rauch remarked to Tieck, was a result of Schinkel's English experiences which placed high demands on the construction workers, as errors in the execution of the building could not be covered up.

Over four layers of stone followed a layer of lilac-glazed bricks, which interrupted the reddish structure and, by means of their horizontality, emphasized the warehouse character of the entire building and created an overall feeling of calm.

This summary by Rauch, expressed to his friend Tieck and in the presence of the master builder, though not heard by him, was like a hymn to the creator, a song of praise that they could not sing often enough.

Tieck had listened attentively and then said, "It does me good to hear you say that again. You can imagine how proud I am to have made a small contribution when Schinkel commissioned Kiss and me to design the main entrances to the Building Academy and the Oberbaudeputation, each of which is dedicated to important architects and embodies the original organic nature of architecture in a visual language that will hopefully be understood by the public. The terracottas of the window parapets, on the other hand, illustrate scenes from the history of architecture and the various building trades."

Rauch, who had followed his friend's explanation uttered enthusiastically and in a raised voice, smiled approvingly, lightly put his hand on his arm and pointed to the sick man.

"Let us go and leave our sick friend alone. If only we could help him."

When they were at the door, it was opened from outside and the family doctor, accompanied by Madame Schinkel, entered. Rauch seized the opportunity to ask what was wrong with Schinkel's eyes and whether the lack of vision was due to his cerebral palsy or to the eyes themselves.

The doctor sighed and said, "Gentlemen, I can only tell you what I have observed so far. The reasons I can only guess. Probably, however, his sightlessness is due to the affection of his brain. If that is the case, it must have happened before the stroke hit him on September 9th last year. Already when I saw him again three years ago, I was very shocked. In addition to an impure colorite, a cloudy, dirty-yellow conjunctiva, a whitish-slimy coating of the tongue in combination with an epigastrium that was very sensitive to touch, he complained especially of a disturbance in his vision, which caused him to see objects split in a perpendicular direction and to perceive only half of them."

"That's what Gropius told me," Rauch interjected. "When Schinkel spoke to him last September during a walk along Unter den Linden about the plan to re-exhibit the panorama of Palermo that he had shown at the Christmas exhibition in '08, he complained that to his chagrin he could only deal with these things at half strength, because not only was he suffering from migraine-like headaches again, despite his cure in Bad Hofgastein, but he also had difficulties using his right hand and with seeing and focusing. By the way, this was one day before the stroke that forced him to his sickbed."

The doctor, who had followed Rauch's remarks attentively, took up his thought again and continued, "His condition was so apathetic that I could not even figure out which of his eyes was actually responsible for the disorder. Later, after this severe stroke, when he was already lying more or less the way you see him now, the right eye appeared completely insensitive, staying rigidly open even if an object was suddenly brought near, constantly watering, and both eyes proved to be completely insensitive to the stimulus of the light in the pupils, so that we must assume that our patient no longer saw anything at all."

The friends listened to the doctor's report gloomily, said good bye to Susanne and the doctor, took another look at their friend and, without having previously planned, almost automatically headed for the museum. When they were at some distance from the Bauakademie, they stopped, turned around and looked at the building.

"Do you see," Tieck said, "how the façade is structured and is composed all-around of pilaster strips with floor cornices, and the resulting fields each take up a window?"

"Of course I can see that, my friend," Rauch replied, "and I also remember from the time the building was erected how the design of the façade was consistently based on the building structure, a framework of pillars with few walls between which the vaulted ceilings were inserted. A groundbreaking construction principle, which our friend had got to know in England. It can largely do without load-bearing walls, the building stands there for a while like a skeleton, which is then filled to completion. This building, in which the art of building and much that belongs to it is taught and learned, in which Prussia's buildings are planned and designed, this house, in which the spiritus rector of Prussian modern architecture works, but is now at the end of his tether, is a house of building in the fullest sense of the word, a house that harmoniously unites purpose and form, a Bauhaus."

"How right you are," Tieck said. "One sees here clearly that Schinkel is never concerned with an architectural theory of form per se, an architectural doctrine dogmatically laid down in treatises. Schinkel here gets rid of rigid stylistic ties. The arch, for example, is for him neither Roman nor Romanesque, but rather an architectural possibility to plausibly open the wall by cutting it out of the structure and at the same time emphasizing the unity of the whole construction."

"Yes," Rauch said, "you could say that he makes the emotion that this opening triggers in people the subject of his design. And throughout his life, it seems to me now, Schinkel tried to explore this effect of architectural form. Therefore, the accusation that he changed the style according to opportunity is completely unjust, since he made the style the servant of his expressive will, while others let themselves be dominated by it."

"And we must not forget," Tieck continued, "that Schinkel has been accused of having detached himself from the architectural tradition with this Building Academy and thus paved the way for stylistically unrelated, purely technical building in the near and distant future. I think I understand our friend in a completely different way: he probably sensed that the skeleton and the raw brick cube alone endanger the art of building. Hence the Doric column and the cornice on the brick cube. And whoever among the young and new architects now appearing everywhere and believing they have mastered the art of skeleton construction and brick but have not mastered this Schinkelian balance between progressiveness and tradition, is doing great harm to architecture."

"Let me summarize," said Rauch, concluding their conversation, "Schinkel's architectural dimension is completely new, he is the first person who is not interested in forming a new style nor in reviving a historical one. Rather, he is aware of the specifics innate in all construction throughout all styles."

They stood admiringly and thoughtfully for a while, until Tieck said, "Let's take a look at the fresco in the vestibule of the museum. I have long believed that Schinkel portrayed himself here, parting in a boat, the skiff of Charon. For a long time, he had probably felt his strength waning and was inwardly preparing for what he is now suffering. Strange that he never philosophized about death and its consequences for himself. He was, I think, too busy."

After they had been to the museum, they continued their walk, passed the Great Granite Bowl and went down Unter den Linden towards the Brandenburg Gate. After their visit to Schinkel, they did not want to part yet and probably needed the presence of the other to comfort them.

"Do you remember," Rauch said after a few steps, "when the three of us were in Weimar to see Goethe, when was that, in the early 20s?"

"Exactly in 1820", Tieck put in, "and we both wanted to make Goethe's sculpture, and we hadn't told each other anything about it. The old man thought very highly of our friend, and I also had the feeling that he liked very much to be immortalized in this way."

After they had walked together for a while along the promenade Unter den Linden, mostly in silence and lost in their memories, they parted at Grosse Friedrichstrasse.

Rauch was even more depressed than Tieck. He had taken a similar path in life as Schinkel, which brought him very close to his friend. Both had to struggle with great difficulties at the beginning of their careers. They both came to Berlin from the province, went to Italy and to Humboldt in Rome at the same time, and came into contact with the Royal Court early on. Rauch was for a time the valet of Queen Luise, Schinkel furnished a few rooms for the Queen in the year 1810.

And Humboldt gave both of them the decisive direction of their lives: Schinkel became a civil servant, and through Humboldt's mediation Rauch received the honorable commission to make the sarcophagus for the deceased Queen. All this and more went through Rauch's mind as he walked on. Schinkel was a guest at the engagement and wedding of Rauch's daughter Agnes; they celebrated New Year's Eve together and went on excursions. The Crown Prince, interested in art and with a mind above average, often invited both of them to his table or drove with them to Charlottenhof Palace, where they quite frequently stayed overnight.

These memories will remain, even if my friend should pass on, Rauch thought. He was worried about Susanne and the children. What would become of them? Schinkel hadn't amassed wealth, he had often, because of friendship, worked for nothing. He had told him that as superintendent he was paid 2,800 thalers. Fortunately, the King had freed him from paying the rent of 280 thalers for the official residence in the new Bauakademie

Nevertheless, the numerous baths and cures, the not inconsiderable household budget, the duties as a host, the expenses for a befitting appearance did not leave much of the salary despite being careful with the money. In any case, a word will have to be put in with the new king for the financial support of the family. After all, what he had done for the Royal House and the state was inestimable.

CHAPTER 12

On the 1st of June 1840, Bishop Eylert, Rauch and Schinkel stood together when the foundation stone for Rauch's equestrian monument to Frederick the Great was laid at the end of the Unter den Linden promenade.

It was an early summer day, cool and cloudy. The wind blew dust and leaves left over from the fall into the group of several dozen people who attended the celebration. In hushed voices they drew attention to the fact that the King looked down from the corner window of the Palace onto the square for a short time, then disappeared. He was ill, as everyone knew, and certain changes in the course of business had been in effect for days, indicating that he was convinced of his imminent end. The Crown Prince had been ordered to open all letters and documents in the inbox in the Palace every morning, to hear the usual military and civil reports and to put his signature on behalf of the King on the cabinet orders of the day. The dying King desired only to be informed twice a week on the most important matters.

Since a fortune teller in Paris had predicted the year 1840 as the year of his death and, moreover, the White Lady had recently appeared in the Palace, he did not believe that he would survive the year. The year 40 had always been of great significance for the House of Hohenzollern. Friedrich II, "The Iron One", from the House of Hohenzollern followed his father as Elector of Brandenburg in 1440. In 1640 the later Great Elector took over the reign, Frederick the Great had ascended to the throne in 1740, so that decisive events could rightly be expected in 1840, too.

Bishop Eylert told Rauch and Schinkel about the rumors of the reappearance of the White Lady, which had apparently been spread by a valet who claimed he had seen her in a corridor of the Palace while he was on his way to follow the call of nature. He was so frightened that the need had become superfluous; instead at midnight, by candlelight and scared to death, he had cleaned his trousers in the Palace kitchen and, as medicine against his fear, had served himself abundantly from the old cognac intended for the King's dinner party. One of his listeners impolitely asked if he had not drunk the cognac first and then seen the White Lady.

And the Countess Hacke, Lady-in-Waiting to the Crown Princess, reported about a sentry who, waking up from a faint, claimed to have seen something terrible, namely a woman in white veils. Fräulein von Block, Lady-in-Waiting to Princess Karl, claimed to have seen something eerie, too. At a ball in the house of the Prince of Prussia, to which a brilliant assembly of Prussian and foreign notables were invited, a stone is said to have fallen from the ceiling of the hall, barely missing the monarch's feet.

The more urgently the bishop tried to put a stop to the foolish rumors and warned of such superstitions in a recent sermon, the more the Berliners liked to tell the story of the White Lady among themselves, accompanied by gruesome and lustful shivers.

In the murky past when the law of the jungle still ruled all lands, the young but already widowed Countess Agnes lived in the Count's castle in Orlamünde in Thuringia, where the Orla flows into the Saale. She had two small boys, whose guardian was a young knight, Burgrave Friedrich von Hohenzollern. He sometimes came on horseback to look after his wards, and because he was a very handsome gentleman, of noble manners and full of respect for women, the Countess grew very fond of him. When he came to Orlamünde, she always took a warm bath in the large wooden tub, rubbed herself with all kinds of fragrant herbs and essences, put on her most beautiful clothes and adorned herself with jewels from her treasure chest. Moreover, she showed herself so friendly and humble towards him that she won his heart so that he would have liked to marry her. But he was a good and faithful son, and since he realized that his parents were against the marriage, he kept silent and wanted to wait until the revered old folks would change their minds.

Thus, the years passed by, the young man remained silent and apparently as cold as a marble stone towards the beautiful widow, whom he had come to love with all his heart.

It so happened that the deeply grieved woman heard from a monk, who had been her confidant and done all kinds of business for her, that the young burgrave had said that the Countess in Orlamünde was the most beautiful flower of all Germany; but as long as four eyes did not close, he could not make her his wife.

He may have meant his parents by this; but the Countess believed he had had her children in mind. Then Satan entered her heart.

On a stormy night, the cruel mother had her hunter Haider secretly murder the little ones in the dark pine forest. The children, weeping and in fear of death, asked the wild murderer to spare their innocent lives, but in vain.

The degenerate mother even mourned them publicly with many tears and buried them in splendor.

The horrible crime became known and was brought before a secret court, which ordered that at night a chip be cut from Orlamünde castle gate to show her guilt, and also that the Countess was to be punished. Burgrave Friedrich, however, was one of the jurors and was charged with executing the verdict, which was the death penalty. He alone among all the jurors was able to guess the reason for the crime and was now to sacrifice the woman who had loved him more than her own children. But he was a man and a dutiful judge. The Countess fell by his hand.

As a restless shadow and White Lady, she now wandered, announcing disaster, through the houses of those who descended from the man she had loved so much but who had killed her.

The Berliners liked the story immensely, and the men had no doubt that they would be no less manly on a similar occasion.

Schinkel, who knew the story, only listened with half an ear to the remarks of Rauch and the bishop about the White Lady of the Hohenzollern. He had a violent headache and also had difficulty recognizing things around him. The objects sometimes blurred and seemed to him as if in two halves. He was shivering more than the weather suggested, and he felt very depressed. Was it because Rauch's design for the equestrian monument had been accepted despite his objections? Or was it rather the news he had received of the suffering and death of Caspar David Friedrich in Dresden?

In Friedrich's peculiar, always dark and somber temper, possibly a precursor of a brain disease to which he later succumbed, certain morbid ideas had developed which began to completely undermine his daily existence. Suspicious as he was, he tormented himself and his family with thoughts about his wife's fidelity, which were completely unfounded but nevertheless sufficient to absorb him completely. Attacks against his family did not fail to occur and made life troublesome for them. The illness made their already tenuous economic situation more and more desperate.

Then came two strokes, and the year '37 saw him almost completely paralyzed. He gradually sank into mental derangement and died on May 7th that year.

Schinkel hoped to God that He would spare him such a fate, the helplessness and the sickbed. He couldn't imagine anything worse than to face death paralyzed and completely dependent on others.

He thought that the lack of recognition that Frederick's work had met with after the wars against Napoleon had contributed to his illness. Even Goethe, who had visited Friedrich's workshop in 1810 and received the painter the following year in Jena, Goethe, who first acknowledged Friedrich's achievements and praised them highly, later said that one should smash Friedrich's pictures on the corner of a table, such a type of painting should not get about.

Schinkel thought sadly that even a genius like Goethe arrived at judgments that could hardly be reconciled with his usual other aesthetic greatness and showed how much even a genius is a child of his era. But perhaps Friedrich had been too political and believed too much in the power of what many today call progress.

When, after the Congress in Vienna, the conservative-restorative element began to assert itself in Europe, the bitterness of disappointment must have made him ill. The artist's most sacred ideals and the personalities who were his most venerable models faded into the background, and his hope of being able to work steadily and gradually for a national and religious renewal had to be buried.

This hope was still great with his first important painting, "The Cross in the Mountains", painted as an altarpiece for the chapel of Count Thun in Chechnya, although the painting aroused doubters from the very beginning. But there are always doubters, Schinkel thought. It was unusual not to see a biblical scene or religious legend as the main picture above the altar, but a landscape? A natural scene, deeply religiously felt, which invites the viewer, like the painter, to seek God omnipresent in nature.

But still, Friedrich had left behind a great work, and a painting such as "The Chasseur in the Forest" will have deeply touched viewers when those who are now criticizing him will long be gone. But Goethe, though a draughtsman of high rank himself ... He quietly shook his head at this inconsistency.

His King and patron, who was now dying, had liked Friedrich's paintings and had made him a member of the Royal

Prussian Academy of Arts as early as 1810, which, unfortunately, meant little improvement in his livelihood. It is interesting that the King did not know or did not want to know about Friedrich's sympathies for the citizens' struggle for certain liberties and national unity. He supported the restorative efforts of the Viennese Court to the best of his ability, and Schinkel wondered to what extent the fine arts, above all architecture, had been influenced by this. He could not recall if certain projects had been prevented or changed by the King for reasons of politics or ideology. Changes or even cancellations had always been caused by pecuniary scarcity.

He looked around, looked at his museum, the Packhof warehouse, the Guard House, the Bauakademie, the Friedrichwerdersche Kirche, the cathedral, the whole ensemble of buildings created or modified by him, which gave this central part of Berlin its character. Building in a city is urban design, and this should be subordinated to a corresponding aesthetic effect and certain principles of perception, i. e. it should enable organic growth, but by no means unconditionally obey the artificial needs of the new age.

Organic growth under the careful hand of the architect finally results in the regular whole, the organism, as he had planned it with reference to the four most significant components, the river, the island, the great road and the great building, and sent his plan to the King in Teplice in July '28. Just as from the Unter den Linden promenade, from the arsenal, the cathedral dome could appear as the end point of the great street, so conversely from the cathedral portal the view had to open up to the beginning of this street and the east-west central axis with the greenery thus presented as an element extending beyond the square.

In the same way, as in the Jardin du Luxembourg in Paris, with the exquisite view of the Pantheon, the connection between the Palace, the street Unter den Linden and the Brandenburg Gate was to be emphasized. This was to be achieved by a large fountain in front of the Palace, which was placed exactly on the central axis of the Unter den Linden and at the same time stood in relation to the central axis of the museum and the large lawn.

A fountain in the middle of the square, Schinkel had written, would make a nice point de vue for the street from the Brandenburg Gate.

The King rejected the plan, and Schinkel once again had to make a virtue of necessity and restored the square in such a way that it could still be considered beautiful, although the overall cityscape was neglected.

Nevertheless, he was not unhappy with his King, who had become dear to him because of his sense of duty, his penchant for the simple life and also his consistent attitude of mind, which Schinkel did not always share. Now he was dying, the Crown Prince would follow him on the throne, and then they would build together. At least that was what His Royal Highness had announced.

Schinkel felt weak and had given up on great hopes. His strength had dwindled, and he was not sure whether he would be able to cope with the conflicts arising from the medieval-romantic views of the Crown Prince in the long run.

All in all, working with the present King had been satisfying and successful and had forced him, the architect, to arrive at some fruitful thoughts by curbing his imagination.

The King, who was born in 1770 and was sixteen years old when Frederick the Great died, spanned several epochs. As a young man he experienced the Ancien Régime, then the revolution in France and finally the Wars of Liberation against Napoleon.

At the end of the wars, he promised the people a constitution and the representation of the people, but only managed to get provincial parliaments summoned in '23. Schinkel had no doubts about what the persecution of the so-called demagogic activities and the restriction on the freedom of the press meant for many upright men. And yet he felt close to the King, who abhorred the political excitement concerning matters which he thought most people did not understand.

Among the workmen who had been employed in the construction of the Bauakademie, Schinkel had a wild carpenter named Burghardt, an outspoken enemy of the monarchy and fighter for the emancipation of the Third Estate. This Burghardt had succumbed to political hysteria, in which he imagined himself to be always right, to have a talent for holding to opinions once they had been formed despite their clashing with reality. No, with such people, who were against police violence and censorship only when they were directed against themselves, one couldn't find common ground, but he saw the time was not far off when they would get the upper hand. And once they ruled the state, they would always subordinate themselves to their customary Teutonic behavior and do everything to ensure that the possibility of subordination would not be taken away from them again.

The ceremony of laying the foundation stone had meanwhile come to an end. The military band played "Hail to Thee in Victor's Crown", then Schinkel said goodbye to his two friends and made his way home to the Bauakademie. The zoning plan for the Moabit district had to be completed.

CHAPTER 13

How my back hurts me when I move because the sheet sticks to the sore spots. Why doesn't the doctor do anything about it, why can't I tell him? They pester me with food and force me to drink and don't see and I cannot tell them that I want to be left alone.

Susanne, dearest, do you remember when I recited Goethe's poem to you on our trip to Italy, which was made possible by His Majesty's stipend on the occasion of the happy completion of the museum? Kennst du das Land wo die Zitronen blühn?

Oh, could we move there again. Leave the King, the Crown Prince, all the people who want something from me, and just go away with you and the children.

Italy. I know that even there I couldn't stop drawing, writing, studying, comparing. You bore it patiently, my dear wife. The architecture of Italy had to be studied, already on my first trip with Steinmeyer, especially in view of the construction of the residential buildings in Naples, some things had come to my mind that reminded me when building to pay closer attention to the interrelationships between location, climate, available building material and the character of the people.

For Prussia one day, the Neapolitan experience would serve me well. The prerequisite for all design is craftsmanship; this means that the separation between art and craft must be overcome. The ultimate goal of all artistic activity is the building, the total work of art, which all the arts must serve together. A new unity of pure art and useful arts is to be striven

149

for in all areas concerning construction. In this way, architecture becomes an expression of the unity of artistry and humanity.

Will I rise again from this bed and into this life? Do I still want it? Let me be, since my pain is very great, often unbearable. Let me go, my dearest, and when we meet one day in heaven, I will call you by your name and you will be mine forever.

A bedsore or decubitus ulcer is a gangrenous death of the skin in places that are exposed to prolonged pressure and is caused by inadequate blood circulation in the compressed areas, also by the nerve activity being reduced and the blood quality being insufficient to nourish the tissue. Bedsore is common with patients who have to lie on the same spot for a long time, especially in the region of the sacrum, on the large rolling hills of the buttocks, on the heels, less frequently in the area of the shoulder blades, that is, in places with little fat padding and located directly above the bones. The fastest and worst development the bedsore takes in connection with debilitating diseases. After initial reddening, an ulcer forms on the affected area of the skin, which usually spreads and deepens accompanied by strong pain, sometimes becoming very large. It can lead to death. For prevention, frequent changes of position are necessary, if possible; the sheets must be smooth and without wrinkles. It is important that the threatened areas are kept clean and frequently checked. If already reddened, they should be washed more often during the day with camphor alcohol and protected with lead plaster.

Dr. Pätsch had initially overlooked the reddened spots, distracted by the other symptoms, the ulcers in the neck, the necessary bleeding and cupping, the difficulties of feeding and cleansing the sick person.

As a result of the bleeding the patient had regained a certain ability to communicate. He expressed pain in individual sounds and words. He braced himself with hands and feet against the painful procedure of cupping. It turned out that he used his right hand less forcefully than his left, he pushed backwards with all the weight of his body to get back into a lying position, and it was difficult to keep him seated.

By the time the doctor became aware of the decubitus ulcer on the patient's back it was too late, and he could no longer heal the wounds that had formed.

Pätsch had studied special pathology and therapy with Hufeland, worked under him at the Charité hospital in Berlin and received clinical training. Like his teacher, he did not think much of the emerging percussion and auscultation, so that he did not use them for diagnosis in the case of this patient.

He remembered that Hufeland once told him about one of the famous Friday parties at Goethe's house, where he had read from his notes on organic life, the summary of which read: "Human life, when viewed physically, is a peculiar, animal-chemical operation. Like any operation, it can be promoted or hindered, accelerated or retarded. Now the science that establishes and summarizes the rules of dietary and medical treatment of life in order to prolong it is macrobiotics. Ordinary medicine pursues other purposes and therefore must not be confused with it. The purpose of medicine is health, the purpose of macrobiotics is long life.

Nice, thought Pätsch, only that a long life without health is hardly attainable, nor is it desirable. He looked at his patient with sadness, who would no longer be able to profit much from the advancements of medicine. Privy Councilor Goethe was quite right when he said: "Our life can certainly not be prolonged, not even by a day through the doctors. We live as long as God wills; but there is a difference between living miserably like poor dogs and living well and fresh, and a wise doctor can do much about that."

Then he was probably not a wise doctor when he looked at his patient, who was wasting away so awfully. If he had been able to give him medical advice earlier and if the patient had followed that advice his condition might now be different. But the ifs do not contribute much to the correct medical way of thinking.

He turned back to the sick man and immediately decided to lift him out of bed with the help of Madame Schinkel and her daughter, to apply lead plaster to the places where he had the wounds and to change the linen sheet. In this way he could perhaps relieve his deplorable condition a little.

All this was shortly after Thorvaldsen had visited the patient, and he had obviously recognized him by his voice.

Come closer, dear friend and thank you for your sympathy. But I must confess to you that I do not at all appreciate some of your works. What everyone praised to heaven as a pure reincarnation of antiquity seems to me cold and dry. But we are similar in one aspect, in a kind of feverish intensity of work, as you showed in your work on the Alexander Frieze in the Palazzo del Quirinale in Rome, which you modeled in only three months, albeit in anticipation and honor of the oppressor of the people. But about your Christ figure, Christus Consolator, we'd better be silent.

Thorvaldsen saw the sick man's lips move, he looked into eyes that could not see him, and had to turn away and leave the room, because the misery overwhelmed him. Outside, he let his tears run freely for the greatest architect of the century, the most extraordinary Karl Friedrich Schinkel, who outshone his contemporaries beyond all measure, and who lay there so utterly helpless.

Why are you leaving so quickly, Thorvaldsen? I have to tell you about Orianda. It's true that the Crown Prince's sketch was preferable to my design of a large, defiant castle with four round corner towers in Russian style. I made the sketch of His Royal Highness the basis for my designs.

It had begun with the wish of Her Imperial Majesty the Tsarina Alexandra Feodorovna, eldest daughter of our King. As she was ailing, she wanted a castle in the warm climate of the Crimea in the sublime style of pure Greek art rejecting any foreign element. But this ideal style couldn't be reconciled easily with the modern living conditions, so it had to be modified. This commission, which required a lot of perspectival and architectural drawings, would have given me even more pleasure if it had fallen into a healthy period of my life. But the way things were, I had to fight many battles with myself in order to stick to it without long interruptions. The great hope to realize freely such a project and to summarize all my experiences and plans made me overcome the illness only temporarily.

I didn't succeed in designing the desired simple summer residence. I had to draw, paint and design an oriental fairy-tale castle, as I simply could not help but take advantage of this perhaps last opportunity. Water features and columns with ribbons decorate the inner courtyard. The terrace in front of the caryatid portico allows a view over the sea. The magnificent open location on a picturesque height is a charming seduction to tempt the spirit to wander outside all the time. The symmetrical plan is aligned with the landscape at the bottom. Entering through a portico flanked by service blocks, I let the visitor pass through the great formal atrium to the vast enclosed Imperial Court or Garden, in the center of which is a tall podium planted with trees and carrying a pavilion in the form of an Ionic temple. Incorporating plate glass panels which would make it almost transparent, it appears to float above the rest of the palace.

This temple is indispensably the crowning glory of the whole building, and it interrupts the simple long lines of Greek architecture in a picturesque way.

I want to use the substructure as a cool promenade, like a grotto, which I will make more attractive by creating a museum of the Crimea and all the classical provinces along the Caucasus in it, so that one can enjoy the works of ancient art while walking along.

Magic, warmth and hope for a better country are conveyed in the inner courtyard. Gilded metal roof tiles show the wanderer from afar that the most powerful imperial house on earth has a residence here.

Once in a lifetime something great must be built, free from all conditions of utility, serving a higher transcendental purpose, beauty and imagination by dreaming architecture and showing what man is capable of ...

The doctor tried, as he did every day, to get the sick person to speak, to react, although he realized that the spiritual life was more or less extinct. Together with the expressions of his unwillingness to suffer pain or discomfort, all other expressions of will ceased, and none of the usual stimuli, such as addresses, questions, attempts at feeding or giving drink, were of any avail.

Even small events like showing the tongue or offering his hand were rare and sometimes didn't occur for weeks, and when they did, they spread great and ever new joy in the family, which soon gave way to horror when Schinkel was seized by the most violent brain spasms. Under strong congestions of the head and chest, the facial features were convulsively distorted, all, even the paralyzed limbs, were violently shaken, the breath faltered, and all this made one fear sudden death. The cramps wouldn't stop, but broke out with even greater force, light red blood flowed from the bruised tongue, the whole body was dripping with sweat and the blue-colored glowing face appeared swollen to the point of bursting.

The doctor finally had to reach for the lancet. But before the second cup was filled, the cramps stopped.

Very strange was the nature of the blood released from the vein; seven eighths of the cup was filled with a turbid, greenish-yellowish serum, and the bottom eighth contained a blackish-bluish liquid without any coherence. These signs indicated that the blood production must have been affected in a peculiar way, probably also as a result of pathological innervation.

Moreover, from then on, the patient refused food and drink completely, so that there was a rapid decline in strength, and death was to be expected.

The image came closer, became clearer, and he could complete the dove. Hurriedly, in fear that it might elude him again, he set the black dot for the eye, and then suddenly the arms let go of him so that he, finally free, staggered into the picture. Breathing heavily, he leaned against the tree in the middle.

In front of him the stream shone, a soft wind blew from the blue sky, and the deer turned his head to the right, towards him. He shaded his eyes with his hand and looked into the blue distance, where, freed from the oppressive constraints of the present, Orianda rose, the result of his art and unbridled imagination. He carefully walked down the path to the riverbank, holding on to the railing, even though headache and dizziness had passed. He set his foot on the water that carried him and, hurrying off he disappeared into the hazy distance and became one with the castle.

> Yesterday, October 9th, 1841, after a long illness, Karl Friedrich Schinkel, Professor of the Royal Academy, died. Except for a few moments of awareness, he did not awake from the unconsciousness into which he had fallen on September 9th last year.
> (Königlich privilegierte Berlinische Zeitung of October 10th, 1841)

Epilog

Schinkel was buried on the 12th of October, 1841, in the cemetery of the Dorotheenstädtische Gemeinde in front of the Oranienburger Tor. The coffin was followed by an endless crowd of people who, in deep mourning and incredulous amazement, refused to believe that Schinkel should no longer be among them. It seemed as if they had to make sure by their participation that this was the case. Many could not hold back their tears, because the story of his suffering, which had been the talk of the whole city of Berlin, had touched them to the heart. One year later, a tomb for him was erected in the cemetery, a replica of a monument he had designed himself. This followed Beuth's advice, who had repeatedly stated that no better monument could be given to the deceased than his own work.

Schinkel's wife Susanne died on the 29th of May, 1861, at the age of 80. A part of the official residence in the Bauakademie had been given to her as an apartment for life. The remaining part of the apartment of originally 600 square meters, which consisted of three large rooms, two study rooms of the deceased and a room at the entrance, was reserved for the Schinkel Museum. The King bought Schinkel's artistic estate and the collection of antique plaster casts from the widow for 30,000 thalers.

Schinkel's son Karl studied forestry and eventually became head forester. Of Schinkel's three daughters, only Elisabeth, called "Lieschen", married. She became the wife of the Prussian government assessor Karl August Alfred Freiherr von Wolzogen, who later published Schinkel's writings, not without having made certain changes, however.

Peter Christian Wilhelm Beuth, Schinkel's best friend, whom he had called his "Urfreund", outlived Schinkel by 12 years and died in 1853. He was called the "Father of Prussian commerce" having contributed significantly to the upswing that Prussian industry experienced after 1815. From 1819 Beuth was, among other things, director of the "Department of Manufacturing, Trade and Construction", of which Schinkel had been a member, and headed the General Building School.

Clemens Brentano, romantic poet, friend and admirer of Schinkel, brother of Bettina von Arnim, wrote poems, plays, stories and published with Achim von Arnim the folk song collection "The Boy's Magic Horn, Old German Songs" ("Des Knaben Wunderhorn" 1806-1808).

In Berlin, Brentano underwent a profound religious transformation; the latter part of his life he actively engaged in promoting the Catholic faith. Brentano died one year after Schinkel at the age of 64.

The Crown Prince, since 1840 King Friedrich Wilhelm IV, cultivated the memory of Schinkel by having some of his building projects completed according to Schinkel's designs. In 1841 he arranged for the foundation of the "Zentraler Dombau-Verein" (Central Cathedral Construction Association") by Cologne citizens and in 1842 laid the foundation stone for further construction. In 1880, Cologne Cathedral was completed.

In 1943, the building was heavily damaged by bombs, but remained standing in an otherwise almost completely flattened city. The twin spires were an easily recognizable navigational landmark for Allied aircraft bombing.

In the political sphere, Frederick William IV mitigated some of the measures his father had taken in the pursuit of the Carlsbad resolutions, pardoned a number of people convicted of political offenses, reinstated Ernst Moritz Arndt in his professorship in Bonn and acknowledged his father's promise to give the country a constitution. On the other hand, he was dominated by an exaggerated idea of his royal power. Only the revolution of March 1848 forced him to reforms. Suffering from a brain disease in late summer 1857, which led to increasingly severe memory and speech disorders, he transferred the government to his brother Wilhelm, the later Kaiser Wilhelm I.

Schinkel's friend and patron died in 1861 at the age of 66 in Sanssouci.

Karl Wilhelm Gropius, admirer and friend of Schinkel, died in 1870 at the age of 70 years. Gropius is considered the founder of artistic decorative painting and became Inspector of the Schauspielhaus theater.

Christian Daniel Rauch, connected with Schinkel through friendship and cooperation, was one of the best-known sculptors of his time. Among his most famous works is the monument to Frederick the Great in Berlin Unter den Linden, which was unveiled in 1851. Here, his outstanding skill in monumental and at the same time realistic portraiture is evident. Rauch died in 1857 at the age of 80 in Dresden.

Christian Friedrich Tieck, friend of Rauch and Schinkel, brother of the romantic writer Johann Ludwig Tieck, entrusted with the decoration of the new palace in Weimar in 1801, professor at the Academy in Berlin since 1820, created, among many other things, the groups of horse tamers cast in bronze for the superstructure of Schinkel's Das Alte Museum. He also made a statue of Schinkel for the museum's vestibule. Tieck died in Berlin in 1851 at the age of 75.

The Oberbaudeputation, The Royal Office of Works, formed in 1804 from the Royal Building Department, was the supreme central authority in Prussian construction, without whose approval no state construction could be started. The Building Councilors formed the collegium which had to make all decisions unanimously. The respective Building Councilor had the right and the duty to carry out local inspections and, if he found inadequate execution or gross deviations from the approved plans, to have the construction process stopped. In such cases, since 1822, the executing architects, government building officers and provincial building officials had been threatened with having to bear the costs incurred themselves.

A few years after Schinkel's death, the Oberbaudeputation was dissolved. The close connection between Schinkel's person and the institution was the key to its functioning and effectiveness, which was no longer the case under the leadership of his successor Günther.

The Bauakademie, also known as the Allgemeine Bauschule, built by Schinkel between 1832 and 1836 on the Kupfergraben between the Friedrichswerdersche Kirche and the Berliner Schloss Palace, was the first serial building in the world and the first secular raw brick building in Prussia. The Bauakademie was Schinkel's most forward-looking work. Due to construction of its load-bearing columns and non-load-bearing wall elements, it was a forerunner of the modern skeleton construction method.

On 3 February 1945, the Bauakademie was damaged by bombs and burned out inside. At first it was rebuilt. When 90% of the building had been completed and 3 million marks spent, it was demolished at the beginning of the 1960s as a consequence of the "Socialist Redevelopment of the Center of the Capital of the German Democratic Republic, Berlin".

In 1995, the building of the Ministry of Foreign Affairs of East Germany was demolished in order to recreate the Werderscher Markt area. Since then, proposals to rebuild Schinkel's Bauakademie have been discussed with city and Federal authorities. Between 2000 and 2001 students erected a temporary structure to give an impression of the volume and form of the building. Current proposals under consideration intend to use a reconstructed Bauakademie to accommodate a museum of architecture.

ABOUT THE AUTHOR

Christoph Werner was born in the East German city of Halle on the Saale river and raised as the son of a Lutheran minister. He studied English and German at Martin Luther University at Halle and worked at various universities in East and West Germany before retiring to live in Weimar.

He has written four novels and numerous short stories and essays.

ALSO BY CHRISTOPH WERNER

SHADOWS OF MY FATHER
THE MEMOIRS OF MARTIN LUTHER'S SON

A Novel

Translated by Michael Leonard

An enthralling and original novel that brings to life one of Christianity's most significant figures, Martin Luther, and the tumultuous world of late medieval Germany that shaped him—and was reshaped by him—told by his youngest son, Paul.

Unwilling to join his father's fanatical disciples, Paul became critical of his famous father's critiques and instead turned his interest and intellect to science and medicine. Yet Martin Luther remained a presence that haunted Paul's life and transformed his world.

Shadows of My Father paints a vivid and atmospheric picture of Martin Luther, including his day-to-day life, his break with the Catholic Church, and his singular dedication in sustaining the Reformation. It is also a portrait of a son raised in a harsh religious household who turns his faith to saving lives instead of souls, eventually becoming a royal doctor.

Harper Legend 2017
ISBN: 978-0062846525 (Paperback)
eBook available

TO LIVE IN ALL ETERNITY
Caspar David Friedrich and
Joseph Mallord William Turner

A Novel

Edited by Michael Leonard

Caspar David Friedrich's dark, melancholic view of life and Joseph Mallard William Turner's full-blooded engagement with the world around him characterize this novel. Despite the contrast between them, these two romantic painters are connected by the uniqueness of their art.

Friedrich's works became part of an existential awareness of life. Turner, with his powerful use of light and color, paved the way for a new impressionistic art form.

The novel lets the reader experience an encounter of intimate distance between the two painters and opens the world of their images, their motives and their times.

Tredition 2019
ISBN 978-3-7497-1975-4 (Paperback)
eBook available

LIFTING THE IRON CURTAIN
Tales of a Bygone Country

Edited by Michael Leonard

Much has been written about socialism but very little about what it was like to live as an ordinary citizen under socialism in East Germany. With the fall of the Berlin Wall now 30 years past, the realities of that time have begun to fade. Some people have even become nostalgic, such as former Party functionaries and others who benefited from the communist rule. For the rest, however, it is important to bear witness to what it was really like to live in those times before the memories begin to vanish.

The stories in this book are by their nature far from complete because memory is not linear but impressionistic. Still, the reader may find them of interest because they are the legacy of a lost socialist world.

Tredition 2020
ISBN: 978-3-7497-8132-4 (Paperback)
eBook available

BOOKS BY CHRISTOPH WERNER

Der Bronstein-Defekt und andere Geschichten

Schloss am Strom. Die Geschichte vom Leben und Sterben des Baumeisters Karl Friedrich Schinkel. Roman

Castle by the River. The Life and Death of Karl Friedrich Schinkel, Painter and Master Builder. A Novel

Um ewig einst zu leben. Caspar David Friedrich und Joseph Mallord William Turner. Roman

To Live in all Eternity. Caspar David Friedrich and Joseph Mallord William Turner. A Novel

Buckingham Palace. Roman

Wintermorgen — Geschichten und Geschichtliches

Paulus Luther. Sein Leben von ihm selbst aufgeschrieben. Wahrhaftiger Roman

Shadows of My Father. The Memoirs of Martin Luther's Son. A Novel

Mitgelaufen. (Geschichten aus einem untergegangenen Land)

Lifting the Iron Curtain. Tales of a Bygone Country

Zeitfracht Medien GmbH
Ferdinand-Jühlke-Straße 7
99095 Erfurt, Deutschland
produktsicherheit@kolibri360.de